)oubt flooded her features. "If I even *can* dance, that is."

"Baby, you definitely can. Let me show you."

Still, Andi hesitated, but not for long. A few seconds at most passed before that stubborn gleam hit her eyes, and she nodded again. Carefully, she pushed out of her chair and stood, reached for his hand and, ignoring her cane, allowed him to lead her to the center of the enclosed area. To the dance floor, where there were already several people dancing. "I'm nervous," she admitted in a low, barely audible voice. "I don't want to fall."

"I won't let you fall." Whether it was fate or coincidence or something else entirely, he couldn't say, but the band finished their upbeat song and moved on to a slower one. A song meant for couples. And finally, Ryan pulled this woman he worried about, thought about, wondered about... ireamed of, into his arms. "Trust me on that, if nothing else."

The Colorado Fosters:
They'd do anything for each other...

007029777 U

FROM GOOD GUY
TO GROOM

BY
TRACY MADISON

MILLS &
BOON

First Published in Great Britain 2016
By Mills & Boon, an imprint of HarperCollins*Publishers*
1 London Bridge Street, London, SE1 9GF

© 2016 Tracy Leigh Ritts

ISBN: 978-0-263-91997-4

23-0616

Our policy is to use papers that are natural, renewable and recyclable products and made from wood grown in sustainable forests. The logging and manufacturing processes conform to the legal environmental regulations of the country of origin.

Printed and bound in Spain
by CPI, Barcelona

Tracy Madison is an award-winning author who makes her home in northwestern Ohio. As a wife and a mother, her days are filled with love, laughter and many cups of coffee. She often spends her nights awake and at the keyboard, bringing her characters to life and leading them toward their well-deserved happily-ever-after, one word at a time. Tracy loves to hear from readers. You can reach her at tracy@tracymadison.com.

To the many good guys I am fortunate enough
to have in my life. You fill my world with light.

Prologue

Chaos. Panic. Screams of terror.

Huffing short, heavy breaths, Andrea Caputo used her hands as leverage to push herself across the hard, cold floor, trying to get out of the line of fire. How many others had been shot? She didn't know, could barely see—let alone think—due to the pain exploding throughout her entire right leg. One bullet to the femur, she guessed, and one to the tibia.

Both bones were likely shattered, and, due to the amount of blood, one of those bullets had hit an artery. Which meant she was in even more trouble.

If she made it through this moment of pure hell, her future would include several surgeries, a long recovery and months, if not years, of physical therapy. And Lord, she'd take it all. Happily. If only she survived long enough to get there. *Please let me survive.*

Okay. Okay. In order to survive, she had to get out of the damn hallway and into the closest trauma room, where she'd call 911. Chances were high that someone had already made the call, but what if everyone else thought the same and help wasn't on the way?

The madman with the gun would continue to shoot his way through the trauma center until doctors and nurses and patients alike were dead. Unfair, maybe, to characterize an out-of-his-mind bereaved husband who blamed the hospital for his wife's death and was now hell-bent on retribution as a madman, but with the blood, bedlam and horror engulfing the ER, the title fit.

Another booming shot. Another scream.

Not right. This wasn't right. Juliana Memorial Hospital was, at its happiest, a place for healing and miracles, and, at its saddest, where people said goodbye to their loved ones. As a trauma nurse, Andi had experienced hectic shifts, slow shifts, heartbreaking moments and peaceful ones. After five years, she'd thought she'd seen it all. But this…this was a battlefield.

Why couldn't she move faster? Focusing on the trauma room to her right, Andi fought against the dizziness and the fear that consumed her, and pulled together every ounce of strength she could to breach the few feet that lay between her and what she hoped would prove to be safe ground.

Please, please let this stop.

Now in the otherwise empty room, Andi reached for the bottom of the privacy curtain and yanked hard, sliding it about halfway across the bar before her strength evaporated. Good enough. It would have to be good enough. She didn't have much left in her.

She fumbled for her phone, hit 911 and Send, and tried not to think of all the people around her who were hurt—possibly worse than she was—or dead. Tried not to remember the look on the attending physician's face in the seconds before a bullet tore into his stomach.

Andi had not been able to help.

She'd tried. Her training and instinct had overtaken her shock and her fear, and she'd rushed toward the fallen doctor—her friend—but she'd gone down just as fast as he had, when the gunman turned on her and fired twice in quick succession. Andi didn't know if he'd been aiming for her leg or if she'd simply been moving too fast for a direct hit to her chest or, like Hugh, her stomach. Didn't matter. What did was that she hadn't been able to get to Hugh, hadn't even had the slimmest opportunity to try to save him.

In that group of minutes following her collapse, she didn't remember anything except the seemingly endless screaming, the blast of gunfire, the excruciating pain that enveloped her leg and, within seconds, had magnified and was pulsating throughout her entire body. Pain like she'd never experienced before. Dizziness, blurred vision and then, for a blessed minute, numbness took over. Believe it or not, that was what got her moving again.

Numb was bad. Numb meant she was losing too much blood.

She'd looked at Hugh, whose prone body was several feet from where she'd been shot, and had made a decision. But what if she'd been wrong in her assessment? What if…? No. Surely, she'd been correct, that his pallor, unmoving chest and closed eyes meant that Hugh had bled out. Fast. Surely, he was already gone. She hadn't left a dying man alone, had she?

No. She couldn't think about that possibility now. Couldn't.

Unreal. No. *Surreal.* Impossible that Hugh was dead. Impossible that such violence was happening in *her* hospital. Impossible that she'd been shot, and that others were hurt and dying around her. Impossible that she couldn't do her job, what she was born to do, and try to help the injured. The most impossible of all, though, were the loud cracks of gunfire that continued to blast through Juliana Memorial Hospital's trauma center. When would he stop?

When would someone stop him?

"Nine-one-one, what is your emergency?" The voice, solid and sure and offering hope, slipped into the dense fog of Andi's fear, her panic and disbelief.

"My name is Andrea Caputo and I'm a nurse at Juliana Memorial Hospital," she said in as crisp and clear a manner as possible. "There is a gunman in the emergency room. He's—" she cringed and gasped when the sound of another shot pierced her eardrums "—the widower of a patient we lost yesterday, and…and…people are hurt. People are dying. Send help."

"Help is already there," the female voice said. "Are you hurt?"

"I am. I think an artery was hit by…by the bullet, but if I can stanch the bleeding, I should be… I…I need to… to—" Words, thoughts…everything trailed off as black edged into Andi's vision. She blinked, tried to force her brain to function, tried to stay conscious against the promise of painless oblivion. But the pull was just too appealing, and she started to sink.

"Andrea! Talk to me," the operator said. "What do you need to do to stanch the bleeding? You're a nurse, right? Walk me through the steps."

The sharp command served to momentarily bring her to her senses. "I need to… A tourniquet would do it," she mumbled. "There are supplies here. I just need to…find the strength to get to them. So tired. Just want to close my eyes for a second."

"I have good news," the operator said, her voice calm and collected. "The police have everything under control. You're safe. Where are you in the emergency room, Andrea?"

"Trauma room four. I'm in number four, behind the… um—" what was the word? "—curtain. I'm behind the curtain, on the…um…floor."

"Stay awake just a little longer, Andrea. Can you do that for me?"

She tried. She really did. But the force of keeping her eyes open and her mind alert proved impossible against the weight of her exhaustion. Soothing warmth surrounded her—a pool of tranquility promising relief—and Andi sighed in surrender and closed her eyes.

Chapter One

Afternoon sunlight, bright and bold, saturated the cerulean sky and cast a golden glow on Steamboat Springs, Colorado. Snuggled in a valley, with the majestic Rocky Mountains standing sentry, the pure beauty of the picturesque city should have, if nothing else, brought a smile to Andi's lips. It didn't. Traveling had left her far too exhausted to care.

She craved peace, though, and maybe…just maybe she'd be able to find a grain of that here, miles away from Warwick, Rhode Island, and Juliana Memorial Hospital. Here, in her aunt Margaret and uncle Paul Foster's home, she hoped to regain everything she'd lost. Mobility in her leg, serenity in her heart, a full night's sleep without being awakened by nightmares that echoed with the blast of a shotgun and screams of terror. Pleas for help.

Six months had elapsed since the tragedy that had taken four lives—including Hugh's and the bereaved-husband-turned-crazy-gunman's—and injured twelve others. One-hundred-and-eighty-odd days had passed since Andi had slipped into unconsciousness in trauma room four, mere minutes before help arrived. Due to the 911 operator, she'd been found quickly.

Surgeries were required to put her shattered bones back together, and an infection had set in, causing muscle damage. If she'd been a tad unluckier, she could have lost her leg. Reports to the police and hospital board were given when she could barely think let alone form the appropriate words. Newspaper, magazine and television reporters had called, asking—almost begging—for interviews. Add in the well-meaning but nonstop flood of family and friends and coworkers offering their love, shock and support…well, getting from one minute to the next had proved a herculean effort. So, yes, she was exhausted. To her very soul, even.

She needed to be somewhere she could heal, inside and out.

Oh, her parents and sister were terrific. Ken and Colleen Caputo were loving, devoted parents, and Andrea's younger sister, Audrey, was just as wonderful. The Caputo family enjoyed a close relationship, but Andi had needed…space. They were all just trying too hard.

When Aunt Margaret—Andi's mother's sister—had called and offered respite in Steamboat Springs, the idea had soothed like a salve on a burn. Andi had accepted instantly, and after an early start this morning and two layovers, she'd finally arrived. Yet, she couldn't summon the energy to enjoy the beauty of her surroundings. Tomorrow, maybe.

Her aunt had picked her up from the airport, hugged her close and kissed her cheek, and other than asking how she felt, how her flights were, she had stayed mercifully quiet during their drive. The radio, turned to an easy-listening station, played softly in the background.

For the first portion of the drive, Andi had closed her eyes, breathed and tried to ignore the throbbing in her leg. The remaining portion, she'd just stared out the window.

Now, as they turned into the long, tree-lined drive-way of the large mountain-cabin-style home that Andi had wonderful memories of from a childhood visit, her aunt said, "Here we are, safe and sound. I'll have Paul get your luggage and take it to your room. Are you hungry?"

"I…guess I'm more tired than hungry," Andi said, pressing her fingers against her temples. "But a head-ache seems to be building fast, so maybe—"

"What you need," Margaret said, releasing the key from the ignition, "is a little food, a big glass of lem-onade and a room with no one else in it. Maybe a nap. Don't worry—" she reached over to pat Andi's knee "—I've warned the rest of the family to stay away until Saturday to give you time to settle in and find your bearings. We're having a cookout in your honor."

Bless her aunt for the foresight of holding everyone off. That gave Andi four full days to get used to being here instead of at home. "Thank you. I'm excited, of course, to see my cousins and meet their families, but I'm… Yes, Saturday should be good." And if it wasn't, she'd have to make do. Recalling the email she'd re-ceived yesterday, she said, "Oh. The physical therapist I'll be working with here, Ryan Bradshaw, wants to meet tomorrow. Can you give me a ride or…?"

Important, she knew, to get right back on the healing path, but she wouldn't have minded twenty-four hours of just existing here before jumping back into rehabili-tation. Hopefully, tomorrow's meeting would be more of a question-and-answer session about her treatment up until now. Even though she'd made sure Ryan had received copies of her medical records, he'd have questions. They always did. Sometimes things were missed in the record keeping.

Before Margaret could answer, Paul stepped from the house, his smile wide and welcoming as he almost sprinted toward the car. More greetings. More hugs. More pretending she was normal before she could escape into the solitude she so, so needed right now. Inhaling a large breath, she reached into the backseat for her cane and opened the passenger-side door, forced herself from the car and plastered on her I'm-okay smile.

"Darling! It's so good to see you!" Paul, a tall, lithe man said as he approached her, arms wide open. Ten seconds later, she was embraced in a tight hug. "Been far too long."

"Yes," she said faintly. "Too long. When you visited us in Rhode Island for my parents' anniversary party, I was what…sixteen?"

"Something along those lines." Retreating, he gave her a long look. Nodded. "Go on in. We gave you the guest bedroom on the first floor. Just follow the hallway to the end. Second door on the right. I'll bring in your luggage and leave it outside the door for you to get when you're ready to deal with unpacking. How's that sound?"

"Perfect," she said, again so grateful for the simple yet powerful understanding and acceptance of her aunt and uncle. "Absolutely perfect. I just need a few hours, I think, to—"

"You take as long as you need," Paul said. "Go. Rest. We have all summer to catch up."

Yes, yes they did. Three blissful months to finish repairing all of the damage dealt to her on that cold winter afternoon. Three months to wake up, smell the flowers, see the sun and feel the wind on her face. Three months to…start living again. To feel *real* again.

Steaming hot coffee, toasted everything bagel with butter and cream cheese and the breathtaking—often gut-kicking—view of the Rocky Mountains made for an excellent start to the day. Ryan Bradshaw stretched his legs and sipped his coffee, savored his bagel and congratulated himself on the wisdom of buying this particular property close to three years ago.

The decision to move to Steamboat Springs, Colorado, from Denver had been a surprisingly quick and firm one. His folks had already lived here for some time, and his visits to them had made him realize how he longed for a less hectic daily existence in a place exactly like Steamboat Springs. His thoughts then had been that he'd eventually relocate once he and Leah were married. Unfortunately, their engagement had come to an abrupt end.

The right choice for both of them, but without the glue of their relationship keeping Ryan in Denver, he felt the need to start over somewhere new. And thank God he had, because he had never loved life more. Everything about Steamboat Springs—the views, the people, the lifestyle, the *skiing*—fit him like a well-worn pair of jeans.

Even his zeal for his career had been revitalized, after too many years of fighting burnout. In Denver, he'd worked endless hours for the hospital, with a few private clients on the side when the opportunity presented itself. Here, he'd jumped into the deep end immediately by starting a private practice clinic in this gorgeous house he'd bought.

Due to some fortunate investing over the years, he had the funds to do so, and it hadn't taken long to turn the lower level of the A-frame into a clean, functional therapy clinic. The upstairs of the house—including the deck he now sat at—was his personal living space, and he'd managed to successfully keep the two areas completely separate.

While he still worked more than he probably should, the struggle with becoming overextended had long since faded. A combination of the environment and being his own boss. Oh, he still put in ten to fifteen hours per week at the hospital's rehabilitation unit, but that only made good sense. Doing so allowed him to be a larger part of the community that was now his, and his relationship there gave him access to services and equipment he couldn't easily obtain on his own. A win-win, every way Ryan looked at it. Another plus? He loved what he did.

The mix of his clientele here was much the same as in Denver. Although he did have a greater percentage of folks rehabilitating from sports injuries—skiing, snowboarding, white-water rafting, you name it—he still had those coming out of one surgery or another, fighting illness or disease that had weakened their muscles, or had had an accident that wasn't sports related. Back in Denver, though, his clients had also frequently included trauma survivors.

People who'd survived any type of a vicious, purposeful trauma—Ryan refused to call them victims—tended to require a different type of focus on his part. Sure, every person he worked with demanded his complete attention on their full selves—not just their bodies—but, on the other side of being hurt or almost killed by another's hand, a certain type of shutting down often occurred. In the heart and soul. In the way the world is viewed.

In feeling safe.

Today—in just about an hour now—his first trauma-survivor client in Steamboat Springs would arrive. Andrea Caputo, from Warwick, Rhode Island. A trauma nurse, which could prove challenging on its own, as medical professionals tended to trust their experiences and training over Ryan's, at least in the beginning stages of the relationship. She had witnessed a coworker being shot and killed, and had sustained two gunshot wounds to her upper and lower right leg.

Ryan had thoroughly studied her file. He understood her medical history, as well as her current status, as much as he possibly could from her records. What he didn't know, what he wouldn't know until she arrived and they spent some time together, was her mental and emotional state. This woman had already trekked an arduous road, but she had a hell of a long way to go. She'd need some fortitude, courage and a kick-ass positive attitude to get herself all the way back.

With every one of Ryan's clients, that was always his end goal: to bring them completely back or, when that couldn't happen for physical reasons, as close to complete as was within reach. He hoped, genuinely, this Andrea Caputo was prepared and had already found all the strength she would need. But if not, he'd get her there.

Because that was what he did.

* * *

Andi stared at her feet, unwilling to meet the direct gaze of her new physical therapist. Ryan Bradshaw's dark brown eyes seemed able to see right through her skull and into her brain. She disliked the sensation immediately, even though she knew the feeling bordered on ludicrous. No one could read her thoughts. No one knew what really went on inside her head.

Even a man with penetrating eyes and a demeanor to match.

"I'm sorry," she said softly. "It seems I'm more tired than I realized from yesterday's travel. My…ah…mind isn't functioning properly. Could you please repeat your question?"

"Sure can. I asked about your sleep," Ryan said, his voice low and smooth. "Specifically, how many hours of solid, uninterrupted sleep you're getting each night. Doesn't have to be exact…just give me a ballpark figure."

"Oh. I don't know." Shrugging, Andi lifted her chin and looked straight past the man, to the fluffy white clouds outside the window. "Maybe five? Six?"

The truth hovered closer to the three-hour mark, but her white lie should stop the "What's keeping you awake?" question she preferred not to answer. Her nightmares were hers to battle with and had zilch to do with the physical recovery of her leg.

"Five to six, huh?" Again, *that* look. He didn't argue, though, just scrawled something into her file. Probably that she wasn't that great a liar. He went on to ask her a few questions about her diet, which she answered honestly, and then a more in-depth interview regarding her pain level, where she was at in her daily exercises and how she felt about both.

"How do you think I feel about almost constant throbbing pain and pushing myself to the point of exhaustion every day?" she snapped. She hadn't meant to—not really, anyway—but she was tired of being asked how she *felt*. Not only in regards to her leg, but with everything.

What did it matter how she felt? What had happened, happened. She had two choices: push through and hope to find some semblance of her prior self, her prior life, or...what? Give up, stop fighting, accept this new, frightened version of herself? Never. Never.

"I don't know," he said patiently. Calmly. "That's why I asked."

Unshed tears burned behind her eyes. They wouldn't fall, she knew. She hadn't cried once since last December. But the weight, the fire and the ache of those tears remained. "I'm fine," she said, going for brisk. "I have and will continue to do whatever needs to be done. I think that's what counts, what you should be focused on, and not my *feelings*."

Standing, Ryan closed her file. "That's good to know, Andrea. But my focus is on anything that will help me help you regain strength and mobility. And, yes, in addition to your physical state, that focus includes your mental and emotional well-being. How you feel, what you think. How you're sleeping, and if you're not sleeping well...why?"

Of course. Attitude was a part of the deal. That whole-body-health idea, which Andi had always bought into. Still did, truth be told. But...her attitude wasn't Ryan Bradshaw's business. Or her family's, or her friends' or…anyone outside of her. She'd stuck to that line from day one, mostly because she found burdening others, leaning on others, challenging in the best of circumstances. And this did not fall into the "best of" in any category.

"I'm sorry," she repeated, using her hated cane for stability in order to stand. "I'll discuss my physical rehabilitation with you, be here for our scheduled appointments on time and work my ass off. I'll do whatever you ask as far as exercises and strength training go, and, if deemed necessary, will consult with additional physicians about my future prognosis." Here, she stopped and dragged in a breath, straightened her shoulders and lifted her gaze to his. "But I won't, now or ever, discuss my personal and private emotions or thoughts."

Or her nightmares. Or how a loud noise—*any* loud noise—almost brought her to her knees. Or how she blamed herself for Hugh's death. She should've gotten to him. Should've kept trying to get to him instead of scurrying her own hide to safety. Nicked artery or not.

"That's totally your call, but I won't stop asking."

Obviously, this man had a stubborn streak. Good thing, she supposed, for the type of work he'd chosen. Some remorse crept in for the line she'd drawn so abruptly in the sand. Hell, they'd barely met. Smarter, though, to make sure Ryan understood her barriers from the get-go. They'd be working together twice a week for the entire summer.

"Sure. Ask away, but I won't start answering."

"Hmm. Again, whatever you choose to share is your call. I won't push. But you should know that I'm a very patient man. I'm also very persistent. Especially," he said as he walked toward his office door, "when I have a client's best interest at heart."

A thousand-and-one rebuttals flew to the tip of her tongue, but she swallowed them all. Patient and persistent and stubborn. Well, she'd meet them with her own brand of stubbornness, no problem. Because frankly, the only thing that kept her standing, kept her feeling even a modicum of safety, was keeping her demons to herself. Letting them out seemed dangerous.

Too dangerous. As if her nightmares, fears, inner panic would somehow morph into a two-headed, scaly, ready-to-eat-her-alive monster if she spoke so much as a syllable of them to another soul.

"I suppose we know where each other is coming from," she said, following the path his long, muscular, *functioning* legs had just taken. "When should I be here tomorrow?"

"Same time, but we're not done yet. Need to put those muscles to work before they forget what they're there for." A grin teased at the corners of his mouth, softening the firm line of his jaw and the steady, determined set of his eyes. "You missed yesterday and the day before. As I'm sure you know, forward motion is incredibly important."

"Yes, but I assumed today would be limited to talking and going over a plan. I didn't bring…wear…appropriate clothes and…tomorrow is good enough. One more day won't make that much of a difference. I'm tired and…no. I can't stay any longer today."

She could. She just didn't want to. Not when merely standing so close to this man—a stranger, for crying out loud—had her heart pumping in overdrive and sweat beading down the back of her neck. And a strange fluttering deep in her stomach. All uncomfortable. All unnecessary. By tomorrow, she'd have these reactions tucked away and under control. Hidden beneath the surface, where he wouldn't notice.

"I have clothes you can use, and really, another day makes a huge difference." Angling his arms across his chest, he waited for her to argue or agree. She did neither, just waited right along with him. "I can't force you, Andrea. You have to want to get better."

Damn it. She *did* want to get better.

She just wanted to start the process here in Steamboat Springs tomorrow. After a day of peace and quiet. She yearned to sit on her aunt and uncle's porch and soak up the sun, read a book, get lost in something other than her thoughts, herself. Today, she didn't want to spend another minute thinking about her leg or the long, long road that still lay ahead.

Today, she just wanted to…be normal. Even if she had to pretend.

So, she stuck out her chin and shook her head. "I have every intention of getting better, Mr. Bradshaw. The want is there, don't you worry. But I can't stay any longer this morning. I'm sorry."

He stared at her, and she stared right back. Finally, he nodded and sharp disappointment crossed his features. Why did she hate that? She didn't even know this man. "Okay, Andrea," he said. "I'll let you win this one, but not another. No more skipped days."

"Call me Andi, please. Only my mother refers to me as Andrea, and, sure," she said, hobbling past him, her goal the exit, "no more skipped days. See you tomorrow."

He didn't respond, which was for the better, so she

kept at her slow and steady pace until she'd pushed through the door into the outside. Late-morning sun warmed the top of her head and her shoulders. She breathed in the bordering-on-cool air and tried to release the tension in her muscles, the slight ball of nausea circulating in her stomach, tried desperately to locate that seed of peace that would, once found, grow into a sturdy, towering oak.

No luck. Not yet, anyhow, but maybe tomorrow. Or the next day. Or, hell, in a month or two. She'd get there. She had to.

Sighing, Andi eased herself onto one of the high-seated wooden benches scattered along the smooth stone porch surrounding the lower level of the house and called her aunt, who had dropped her off a little over an hour ago. Margaret had decided to run some errands while Andi did her thing here. She'd offered her the use of her car, but, while Andi had driven once since being given the go-ahead to do so, she still wasn't comfortable with the idea. Her weakened leg worried her, especially here, in a location where she hadn't spent her entire life and did not know the roads, the landmarks or…anything, really.

Yet another goal, one more activity she used to take for granted. Add that to her past ability to sleep fully and soundly pretty much every night, her confidence in herself and, yes, even her place in the world.

Closing her eyes, she sighed again. Truth was, she now knew to never, ever again, take anything in life—from the simple to the complex—for granted.

Chapter Two

"That was excellent work today," Ryan said to Andi the next morning. She'd arrived on time, prepared and—seemingly, anyway—focused. Her refusal yesterday had surprised him. Concerned him some, too, but today proved that on the physical rehabilitation front, her determination was as solid as she'd claimed. He'd put her through the ropes, pushed her a mite harder than he'd even planned, and she hadn't complained once. "I'm impressed."

As to the rest of her rehabilitation, well…he had gained enough experience over the years to know that once they'd worked together for a while, she'd let certain truths slip. Maybe on purpose, maybe by accident, but eventually, he'd learn more about her sleeping habits, her thoughts, how she generally coped in her everyday world. And once he had some idea of those facts, he'd have a much stronger sense of the complete picture. Of how to help, what she needed.

Of what he could do to strengthen more than just her leg.

Shoving a long chunk of damp auburn hair to the

side, she fixed her brown-eyed gaze on him and a small, tentative smile appeared. "Thank you. I think. Tonight, I might be cursing you."

"That's normal. I'd be…shocked if you didn't. We'll take it a little easier next time. Today," he said with a wink, "I wanted to see what you were made of."

She winked back, which came as a nice surprise. It also served as a glimpse—a tiny one, without doubt—of the woman beneath the trauma. The woman she'd once been. Her lips twitched into just about the cutest damn grin Ryan had ever seen before she said, "That's an easy question to answer. I'm made of steel. And now, some plates and screws, not to mention a few intramedullary nails. I think I'm still more human than robot, though!"

In this moment, in addition to the exhaustion, she appeared soft and female, warm and lovely, and a hot wash of attraction suddenly kicked him straight in his gut. Hard and fast and…unexpected. He just hadn't felt that for anyone since Leah. Hadn't wanted to, either.

The fact that he had, out of the blue, for this woman he'd just met—one of his clients, no less—seemed dangerous. Interest lurked there, too. Curiosity. A desire to know more, to investigate and see if his body already knew something his brain hadn't yet locked into.

"Definitely more human than robot," he said, holding his hands out toward her. "Come on now, let's get you up and over to the table so I can massage out the kinks."

Grasping her hands, he helped her stand, making sure he supported her weight until she'd found stability. With his arm around her waist so she wouldn't require her cane, they walked across the room to the massage table. And every step of the way, that buzz in his gut grew stronger and more persistent. More *insistent* that he needed to pay close attention to this woman.

Ryan shook off the sensation and, once Andrea was situated properly, rolled the loose band of her shorts up so he could start at her thigh. "Talk to me," he said as he gently kneaded his fingers into the damaged muscle, knowing even this would cause some discomfort, if not outright pain. "Tell me anything you want. Trivial or important. Just talk, makes this go faster."

Silence enveloped the room, and for a minute Ryan doubted she'd play along. But then, she said, "My aunt is having a barbecue get-together thing on Saturday to welcome me. My cousins and their spouses, kids, will all be there. And all told, there's a lot of them. I don't know my cousins very well. I mean, we're Facebook friends. But…a lot of people. A lot of talking. I'm exhausted just thinking about it." A small, whispery sigh emerged. "Seems pointless."

"What does? The food? Spending time with family?" Ryan had a strong idea of what she meant, but he wanted to see if she'd explain, if she'd let him in that much. "Or maybe you just have a problem with delicious grilled meats and vegetables?"

She laughed and, oh, what a sound. Joyful and spontaneous and…real. Or so Ryan thought, anyway. "I'm actually quite the fan of grilled anything. It's the…questions, I guess. The constant well-meaning questions about what happened, how I'm feeling, and with so many people there, I'll likely have to repeat the same answers a dozen times."

"Make it simple," he said, moving his hands down her leg, applying pressure in gentle yet firm increments as he did. If she winced or showed any sign of too much discomfort, he lightened the pressure. "Just say you'd rather not talk about the incident, but you're feeling stronger every day. Or whatever word you'd prefer. Better. Healthier. Happier. Take your pick. I doubt your family will insist on more explanation than you're willing to give."

"I don't know. I don't know them well enough to say."

"Invite me, then," Ryan said. *Hmm. Where had that come from?* He didn't know, hadn't pre-thought the idea out, but it settled nice enough. "I also happen to be a fan of grilled anything and better yet, I can act as your buffer. Folks will be too curious about me to ask questions."

"Really? You'd do that?" As she spoke, she pulled herself to a sitting position. That was fine, he'd done enough for the moment. Her muscles needed to rest some now. "Must be for the food, because I can't imagine this is a service you offer all of your clients."

"No," he said, wiping his hands on a towel, "acting as a buffer is not a service I typically offer. And it isn't about the food, as good as it will be, I'm sure."

"Then…why?"

"Why ask why?" he said, not sure of the answer himself. Other than he wanted to be there, at Andi's side. Pay attention to his instincts. "Just accept and…invite me to the darn barbecue already. I have Saturday free, surprisingly, which is somewhat unusual as of late."

"You need to tell me why," she said, her voice and shoulders firm. "Because I'm not a…a charity case, and while having a buffer sounds appealing, it certainly isn't necessary."

"I like barbecues. I like meeting new people. Most

of all," he said, while looking her straight in the eyes, "I think we'll have a stronger working relationship if we get to know each other a little better. We'll be at this all summer, Andi. Why not become friends in the process?"

One blink, then another. A slight, somewhat dubious shake of her head. "I know what you're up to. You're still angling to get inside my head. Friends or not, that won't happen. But as long as you can accept that, then why not? You're welcome to come on Saturday."

"Sure thing," he said as he walked over to where they'd left her cane. When he returned with cane in hand, he grinned. "But why don't we set that concern aside for now? Even if I ask you more questions about what goes on inside your head—and I'm likely to at some point—don't forget that you are in control. You never have to tell me anything you don't want to."

"Good. Glad we're on the same page." She slid to the edge of the table and tentatively stood, reached for the cane. "So. Okay, then. I guess I'll see you Saturday."

Hmm. For her to forget their appointment on Friday meant she was rattled on some level, even if her demeanor and voice didn't state so. "Friday first," he reminded her. "Same time, same place. Basically the same regimen, though I plan on making a few alterations."

Light pink coated her cheeks. "Right. Friday first, of course. I…I'll be here." Then, with as much swiftness as she could manage, she made for the exit. Much as she had yesterday.

Sighing, Ryan wiped down the table and, for the moment, put his curiosity and attraction toward Andrea Caputo on the back burner. He had a full day in front of him. His next client, Robert Alvarez, was set to arrive in fifteen minutes. Every bit of his focus had to be centered on work, on his clients' needs and not on a lovely auburn-haired woman who had—in very short order—breathed life into a part of him that he hadn't even realized was asleep.

Interesting. Compelling and curious and, perhaps, somewhat exciting. Descriptions that pretty much summed up the woman herself, at least from Ryan's perspective. Later, when the day was done, he'd give more thought to Andi, to his reaction toward her, and decide what he wanted to do about both. Until then, he had plenty to keep him busy.

Saturday morning dawned bright and sunny, with barely a cloud in the sky. Andrea had hoped for rain. A booming thunderstorm, complete with golf-ball-sized hail. Anything, really, to postpone the barbecue or, better yet, cancel it altogether. Of course, canceling would require a hell of a lot more than your basic thunderstorm.

Armageddon might do the trick.

She'd never been one for socializing with large groups of people, even before last December. Oh, she used to be able to summon the proper amount of energy to appear comfortable, even extroverted, when attending parties, weddings and the like. But she would then require a good chunk of the next day to be by herself to recharge her batteries. Now, though, the very thought of the amount of energy she would need to get through this day flattened her.

Mostly, she just wanted to be left alone in this bedroom with its fluttery white curtains and pretty eyelet bedcover, the walls painted a relaxing, barely blue and the dark, wood furnishings. She wanted to sit in the chair by the window and read a book, listen to some music or maybe doze off. If she could be so lucky.

But that would have to wait for tomorrow.

Sighing, Andi stared in the closet and tried to decide what to wear. Shorts would make the most sense, as the day ahead promised to be a warm one, but between the scars and the loss of muscle tone in her right leg, she would just feel self-conscious. And if she wanted to avoid too many questions, showing off her injuries seemed foolhardy at best.

One of her sundresses, then. Flipping through the half dozen or so she'd brought, she selected the turquoise-and-white tie-dyed dress her mother had bought her last week. The skirt was long—the hem hovering right above her ankles—and the color suited her pale skin and auburn hair. After getting dressed, she slipped on a pair of white sandals, brushed through her hair one last time and touched up her makeup. There. Done.

The slam of a car door outside, followed quickly by another, told her that her family was arriving. Nervous tension turned her stomach upside down, and her palms grew sweaty. Andi closed her eyes, breathed in deeply and reminded herself that these people were here to welcome her, not give her the third degree. They weren't her enemies.

Right. Somewhat sturdier, she grasped her cane and exited the bedroom, hoping that the day would pass quickly and with ease. That some unknown something— a sound, a question, a memory—wouldn't send her into a panic attack in front of her cousins, their spouses and their kids. In front of Ryan, mostly. She should've told him no when he'd invited himself. Had meant to, right on the spot, and again yesterday before their session was over.

Instead, she'd agreed and given him the address. Why, exactly, she wasn't sure, other than his offer had given her a small amount of comfort. Maybe because he was more a known entity at this point in time than any of her cousins and, therefore, increased her overall sense of security. Or maybe it was as simple as he'd said—his presence would decrease the number of questions she'd have to answer—and really, that wasn't nothing. It was a huge something.

Voices from the kitchen emanated down the hallway as Andi slowly made her way. She heard Margaret and Paul talking to another male and female—likely one of their sons and his wife—along with the chatter of a little boy asking about…root beer? She'd made it almost to the threshold when another pair of voices were added to the mix, but this time she recognized her cousin Haley as being one of them. They'd actually spoken on the phone several times recently.

Andi liked Haley. Her comfort level increased tenfold just knowing her female cousin was already here. Even so, she still had to fight the urge to run back to her room and lock the door and burrow herself under the bedcovers. She could do this. It was a barbecue, for crying out loud. Not an execution. If she could remember that, she'd be fine.

Straightening her shoulders, she entered the sunny white-and-yellow kitchen with her trademark, fake-as-margarine smile in place, and said, "Hi, everyone! I think I heard something about root beer? Hoping I did, as I love root beer. It might be my most favorite soda."

"It's mine, too!" said a sandy-haired boy, probably

around five or six years of age. He grinned. "Daddy said that today, since it's a special day, I can drink lots and lots of root beer." Stepping forward, he held out his hand toward Andi. "My name is Henry. I'm almost six!"

"Hi, Henry. My name is Andrea, but most everyone calls me Andi," she said, shaking his hand. This kid amused her in all the best ways. "And really? Almost six? I would've thought you were thirteen, at least. Later, let's have a root beer and talk. You can tell me your secret to staying so young. We can become millionaires together and buy a root beer company!"

"I don't have any secrets! I really am almost six! Sort of. I'm closer to my next birthday than my last birthday, so that counts." Henry scrunched up his mouth and then laughed. "You're teasing, that's all. You didn't really think I was thirteen."

"Maybe not, but I have a feeling you're a lot smarter than the average five-year-old."

"Oh, he is," said a thin-as-a-reed brunette woman, smiling widely at Henry. "Too smart for our own good, most days. It's so nice to meet you, Andi. I'm Chelsea, this little tyke's mom—" she tousled the top of Henry's head "—and Dylan's wife. We've all been looking forward to today."

"Really? That's…nice, and, of course, I'm happy to—"

That was all she got out of her mouth before she was pulled into a tight hug from Dylan, followed by Haley. She barely regained her balance when Reid and Cole, two women and two toddlers swarmed in the back door. And then…well, bedlam.

Talking and laughing, more hugs and more introductions. Through it all, one fact became clear: the Foster siblings weren't only a gregarious group, they were very good-looking specimens of the human race, which naturally, Andi had already known. But seeing them up close and personal for the first time in so many years brought that reality home.

Reid, the eldest, and Cole, the youngest son, greatly resembled their father, with their almost-black hair and eyes, while Dylan, the middle son, and Haley, the youngest of the Foster siblings, took after their mother, with hair very similar in color to Andi's and green eyes. They were a gorgeous crew, no doubt about it.

And she tried—oh, did she ever—to keep up with the jokes, the roughhousing, the mash of chatter that came from every direction, but soon found that impossible. Too many people. Too much noise. It was all just…too much. Easing backward, she leaned against the wall and slowed her breathing, stared at the refrigerator and silently counted to ten. Far too early in the day to allow her anxiety free rein. She wouldn't make it another hour if she did.

Her aunt walked over, stopping in front of her, and placed her hand on her arm, saying, "Honey? Are you okay? You seem a tad overwhelmed."

"A little, maybe, but I'm okay."

"Maybe I should've put this off another week, to give you more time to find your bearings," Margaret said, watching her closely. "If you need to sneak away to be by yourself for a while, do so. No one will think anything of it if you do."

"I will. Right now, I'm just trying to remember everyone's names." She hadn't been, but doing so might be enough to halt her nervous energy.

Moving her gaze around the room, she stopped at

Reid's wife, the pixieish redhead. Daisy? Yes. And their children were the adorable toddler twins, Alexander and Charlotte. Cole was married to the slender blonde with cover-girl beauty. Her name was Rachel. They didn't have any children yet, the same as Haley, who was married to the very tall, very muscular Gavin. Rounding out the group, of course, was Dylan and Chelsea and their son, Henry.

"How'd you do?" Margaret asked. "Need any reminders?"

"Nope. I actually remember all the names." Andi exhaled a breath and some of her tension eased. Of course she could get through the day. So long as she remembered to breathe. "Crazy, huh?"

"Not really. Even as a child, you had an excellent memory. So did your sister."

True enough, Andi supposed, but some things she wished she could forget. "Well," she said, "I'm just glad to have the names down."

Margaret reached up and brushed a strand of hair from Andi's cheek. "You're safe here, my darling. Everyone in this house only wants the best for you. Try to keep that in mind when you start to feel uncomfortable."

"I know. I will."

A sharp whistle cut through the chatter, forcing everyone to turn toward the source—Paul—as he started assigning tasks related to the grill, setting up the outdoor tables and extracurricular activities. Basketball was mentioned, as was horseshoes. It seemed that the barbecue, and everything that went with, was getting started.

Within a matter of seconds, the kitchen emptied of the adult males, and Margaret, stepping away from Andi, exhaled a whoosh of air. "Finally," she said with a chuckle. "Now, I have room to navigate. Haley, can you finish the potato salad? Potatoes are in the fridge, along with everything else you'll need. And Chelsea…if you don't mind, could you and Henry fill the cooler with ice? The cases of soda, water and juice are already out back."

"What else needs done?" asked Rachel, stepping forward.

"Um, let me think." Margaret tapped her finger on her lips. "Oh, the tomatoes, onions and so forth…can you slice those for the burgers? And the barbecue sauce, for the ribs. I need to—"

The doorbell pealed, interrupting Margaret's speech and sending Andi's pulse into overdrive. Ryan had arrived. Suddenly, Andi wished she'd taken a bit more time with her hair, her makeup. Maybe worn some jewelry, and had she sprayed on any perfume?

Oh, Lord. This wasn't a date.

Doing her utmost best to shake off the resurgence of her nerves, she said to the room at large, "That's Ryan. I'll let him in. And then, whatever I can do to help, I'll be more than happy to. Anything at all. Whatever you need!"

"Nope. For one, you're the guest of honor, which mean you won't lift a finger." Margaret's eyes narrowed as if challenging Andi to present an argument. "Also, Ryan hasn't met any of us before and, as a group, we can be a little overwhelming to newcomers. And, sweetheart, he's your guest. Pay attention to him, introduce him to everyone. Mostly, though, just relax and have fun. That is one of the reasons you're here, is it not?"

"Yes, but that doesn't mean—" She broke off as her

aunt's eyes narrowed another degree. "You win. I'll rest on my lazy behind all day while everyone else does all the work."

"Perfect. That's exactly what I want for you." Margaret beamed a smile before pointing toward the front of the house. "Now, go greet your guest before he thinks we're rude and ignoring him."

Nodding, Andi inched her way toward the door and flat out disregarded the zealous pounding in her chest, her once-again damp palms and the swirling excitement permeating her blood. None of that meant anything. Other than that she was nervous, as she had been all week about the barbecue in general. These were symptoms of anxiety, not…attraction or genuine affection.

Couldn't be. She knew almost nothing about Ryan Bradshaw. Besides, for the next three months, he was her physical therapist. The last thing she needed was to mistake his intense focus on her and her well-being as anything other than professional interest and care.

Logical. Rational. Sensible.

Unfortunately, the second she opened the door and laid on eyes on him, her brain stopped thinking. Because, Lord, the man looked good. Dark hair ruffled from the wind, equally dark eyes that seemed to see right through her—filled with warmth and compassion and a type of concentration that Andi felt to her core—and a beaming, bright smile. His jeans fit his long, lean form in such a way that seemed to state they were made for his body alone, and his pale yellow short-sleeved shirt was unbuttoned and untucked, showing the white T-shirt he wore beneath.

Yeah, he looked good. Enough so that Andi realized she just might be in trouble.

* * *

Prickly. Nervous. Uncomfortable. All words Ryan could use to describe Andi's behavior since the second he'd arrived. Whether it was his presence or the gathering in general that had raised her anxiety level, or, he supposed, the combination of both, he couldn't say. But she held her body tense, almost rigid, and while she'd kept up on her end of the conversation with him and various family members, her voice held a forced quality.

She also hadn't truly, freely smiled even once. He liked her smile—her real smile—and wanted to see it again. So, he decided his mission for the rest of the day was to get her to relax enough that she'd be able to smile. Even just once. If he could pull a true-blue laugh from her, as well? Better yet. It seemed of utmost importance to give her a happy, carefree moment.

Several years ago now, his only sibling, his sister Nicole, had been diagnosed with breast cancer. As the disease and the treatment for the disease took its awful, awful toll, one of Ryan's daily goals was to find something—anything—that would make his sister forget what she was going through for enough consecutive seconds to elicit a smile. Or a laugh. Or both.

He did not succeed every day, but he did on most.

Of course, with Nicole, he knew her well enough to have an idea of which tack to take. He did not know Andi well enough, so he'd have to feel his way through and hope he could figure out what might lighten the burden she was presently carrying. He did not have an arsenal of jokes at the ready, so he didn't bother going that route. Rather, he decided to trust his instincts and start with an unconventional approach. Something that might just surprise her enough that she'd let down her guard and start to relax. He wanted her to relax.

Around her family, yes, but mostly around him. He wanted her to eventually learn that she could trust him as her physical therapist and also, hopefully, as her friend. He already knew he liked this woman. Already knew he wanted to learn more about her. And, yeah, he absolutely wanted to see that beautiful smile of hers stretch across her equally beautiful face.

At the moment, they were sitting side by side in lawn chairs under the leafy canopy of a massive tree. Some of the Fosters were playing a game of horseshoes while others were engaged with the kids, and Paul and Margaret were bustling about, starting the meal preparation in earnest. He might as well take his first swing now, see if he could manage a grand slam.

"So," he said, in the most casual voice he could muster, "I have a proposition. Or maybe you'd call it a dare. Either one works, I guess. But if you agree without knowing all of the details, and then follow through, I'll take you out for a night of dancing."

"I don't think you can call that a proposition or a dare if the details of what you want me to do aren't made clear from the beginning." Curiosity and caution lit her gaze, her tone. "Unless you want to play a game of Truth or Dare, but that isn't what you said."

Interesting idea. But…nah. "No, I'm not playing a game. Just want you to step out of your shell a little. Nothing wrong with that, and don't worry, I wouldn't ask you to do anything that I thought you'd find impossible or alarming." He winked. "I'm not going to ask you to streak naked across the backyard or break into song at the top of your lungs. Promise."

Had the corners of her lips wiggled? Maybe. If so, too small a wiggle to say for sure. "That's good, because I wouldn't do either. I might be willing to play along if the reward was something I wanted. But dancing? No. I don't dance. Not anymore. Or not again, anyway."

"Why not? You're certainly capable. I mean, I wouldn't suggest anything too strenuous yet, but so long as you put most of your weight on your left leg, you'd be fine."

"I'd rather not test that supposition," she said. "Therefore, I must decline your offer."

"You know," he said, angling his body toward hers, "I should've explained more. The point of taking you dancing isn't so you can dance. It's so you can see me make a fool out of myself. Because if there is one thing I cannot do, it's dance." He winced. "In fact, my sister says I look like a drunken elephant on ice. And that's one of the kinder descriptions I've heard."

The tiniest fraction of amusement glittered in her eyes. "Is that so? A drunken elephant on ice, huh? Kind of hard to believe, as I've never seen anyone dance that badly."

"Aha! But you can. The sight of such a lack of grace is totally within your power. All you have to do is say, 'Okay, Ryan, I agree. What is it you want me to do?' and then actually follow through on what I ask of you. What do you think?"

"No streaking or singing involved, right?"

He crossed his heart. "That's correct."

Another twitch of her lips, but not a complete smile. Not yet. "Okay, sure. Why not? But remember, I haven't given up the right to decline. Whether I do or don't is totally my choice once I hear what you have in mind. Just so we're absolutely clear on that front."

"I wouldn't have it any other way. This, along with everything else that occurs between us, is one hundred percent in your control. You call the shots, Andi."

She straightened her shoulders, tossed her mane of auburn hair behind one shoulder and jutted her chin. "I'm ready. What do you want me to do?"

"I want you to walk up to any one person here… except for me…and say 'Bugaboo!' three times in a row. Really fast. And in a high-pitched voice. That's it. Easy peasy."

One blink, then another, followed by a third. "Are you insane? Or do you just want my family to think I'm insane? Or—"

"A single word, three times in a row. That's all it is, and you get to choose who you say it to. Come on, Andi, have a little fun. I know you can. Besides which, you really don't want to miss the opportunity of getting me on the dance floor."

"Anyone I want, huh?" She scraped her bottom lip with her teeth as she glanced around the yard. He saw when the obvious answer clicked into place, just as he knew it would. "You have a deal," she said as she stood. "I hope your dancing shoes are polished and ready to go."

"Oh, they are. Go on, do your thing."

She took her time walking across the grassy yard, her cane slowing her movements more than necessary. Truthfully, he doubted she really needed the cane for short walks, but he didn't think she was prepared to give up that security. Soon, though, he'd bring up the possibility.

As he'd guessed, she headed straight for the two toddlers who were presently playing with their mother on a spread-out blanket. Carefully, Andi lowered herself to the ground and held out her arms to Charlotte, who toddled right over. He couldn't hear her from where he sat, so he just watched as she tickled the little girl. Then she leaned in close, assumingly saying "bugaboo" three times, in quick succession and in a high-pitched voice, before tickling her again. Charlotte burst out laughing and then…oh, yes, Andi did, as well.

She turned toward him, her smile spread across her face, and he'd bet money that if he was closer, he'd see that her eyes were filled with joy. She laughed again, the sound easily carrying to his ears, and he heard her happiness, her few seconds of freedom from whatever thoughts and fears swirled in her brain. He was relieved for her. Pleased, too, that he'd found a way to bring her to this moment.

What really got him, though, was how beautiful this woman was. And how very much he wanted to get to know her. Really know her. That, he had no doubt, would be a much steeper hill to climb than simply eliciting a laugh. But he'd figure it out. He'd figure *her* out, and as he did, he'd let her get to know him. Let her figure *him* out.

After all, that was only fair.

Chapter Three

Her heart in her mouth, sweat all but pouring down the back of her neck, Andi woke with a gasp, sat straight up in bed and waited for the worst of the tremors shaking her body to dissipate. Another nightmare. Another return to Juliana Memorial Hospital, seeing Hugh get shot again, her dream forcing her to view the scene over and over and over.

The sound of the gun, the potent smell of desperation and fear, the cries and screams of shock and panic and, yes, the look on Hugh's face as he went down, the magnifying pain when two bullets tore into her leg, and then, when she came around, the belief that her dear friend and mentor was gone and her resulting decision to run. Hide. Save herself. Call for help.

As fresh in her brain as if the incident had occurred within the past five minutes and not six full months ago. When would she move past this? Why hadn't she yet? It frustrated her, this seeming inability to push through to the other side and leave the past where it belonged. What had happened was awful and terrifying, but it was over. *Over.* She'd survived.

But, damn it, part of her heart, her soul, remained stuck. And that needed to change.

Stifling a yawn, Andi carefully swung her legs to the edge of the bed and glanced at the clock, knowing she wouldn't be able to fall back to sleep anytime soon. Three in the morning. Two more hours and she would've actually made the five-hour mark. The first night she did that, she might just throw herself a party to celebrate.

She decided to brew a cup of tea and settle herself in the living room, see if she could find something distracting to watch on the television. Preferably a comedy. Light and silly enough to drag her mind from the darkness of her nightmare. A rerun of *Seinfeld* or *Friends* would be perfect, as one or the other would take her back to worlds and people she knew well.

She didn't find either, but a movie she'd seen before caught her eye, so she paused her search and set the remote down. Why, exactly, she wasn't sure, as *Duplicity* was a romantic thriller. Neither genre suited her current mood. But she kept watching, anyway. Until, that is, it clicked why this particular movie snagged her interest. The male lead, Clive Owen.

Ryan was younger and, naturally, did not have a British accent, but the actor reminded her of him, nonetheless. Some of the resemblance was physical. Their height and their coloring, sure, the cut of the jaw...yes, but it was more than a base likeness in appearance. The two men *moved* their bodies in a similar fashion, and their smiles...they were close, if not exact duplicates.

And watching Clive on-screen made her think of Ryan. Of the day they'd spent together, of how she'd relaxed in his presence and even laughed a few times.

How those damn butterflies in her stomach had come to life when he'd grasped her hand right before he left, before he'd given her that straight-through-her-skull look and told her good-night, that he hoped she slept well. As if he knew, without doubt, that she faced nightmares and insomnia and truly wanted her to rest easy.

Concern and care. Real or imagined? The attraction she felt toward him already…real or imagined? And why, just why, did she just happen across a movie with a deliciously handsome actor who reminded Andi of the man she was trying *not* to think about? Bam, just like that, the flutters were back in force. Oh, hell, no. This would not do at all.

Grabbing the remote again, Andi flipped through the channels until she found a safe, non-butterfly-inducing episode of *The Golden Girls*. She knew plenty about patients developing a—for lack of a better word—*crush* on a caregiver, whether that be doctor, nurse, counselor or, yes, a physical therapist. It happened frequently.

Had happened to her several times, in fact, in her role as a nurse. Anything that could weaken the body—illness, disease, broken bones, surgeries—also weakened the spirit. When enough time was spent with a person who was taking care of you professionally in one way or the other, the spirit naturally became bolstered when in their presence.

In such a situation, feeling attraction—even thinking that love might be waiting in the wings—was a fairly common, if temporary, occurrence.

And while Ryan wasn't her doctor or her nurse, he was still her caregiver. Of a sort, anyhow. Well…maybe the proper description for his role would come in closer to "care helper" than caregiver, but even so, the explanation fit well enough to relax Andi's worries. She didn't know the real man. The real Ryan. She knew the professional who had asked her questions out of compassion and concern the first day they'd met and then had gone out of his way to help her through a tough day. In the long run, her reaction toward him meant nothing.

It was temporary.

Thank goodness she'd recognized this so quickly. Now she'd be able to squash her meaningless *crush* into nonexistence without too much trouble. Heck, she'd recovered from Greg—the guy she'd dated for just shy of a year before being shot at the hospital—breaking her heart in less than twenty-four hours. Easy, really. If he hadn't loved her enough to stick through her recovery, then he obviously was not the man for her. In any way at all.

Different scenarios, yes, but the process? Exactly the same.

But why, oh, why, did her physical therapist have to be sexy, handsome, intelligent, compassionate *and* charming? Really, where was the justice in that?

Sunday afternoon, Ryan drove toward his parents' house, his thoughts on the day before and…of course, Andrea Caputo. Why or how this woman had gotten clean under his skin so fast he didn't have a clue, but he found her in his head more often than not.

Truth be told, the whys didn't concern him nearly as much as what he should do about it. Nothing, for the moment, other than his job and—if he was very lucky— a friendship. A place to build from if there was a reason to, when the timing was better. Didn't he already know the dangers of becoming attached too fast? Yup, he absolutely did.

Leah, the woman he'd planned on marrying, had been his client for close to a year before their relationship began. And in the end—two years and one diamond ring later—she'd walked. She'd been wrong in her feelings toward him, she'd said. A horrible mistake. She loved him, yes, but she wasn't "in" love with him, and while she hoped they could be lifelong friends, she did not want to be his wife. That had smarted some. Like a knife to the eye would.

He understood, though, and appreciated her honesty. Just wished she'd told him of her doubts when they'd first appeared rather than waiting close to another year. He'd had his concerns early on in their relationship, but she'd been so sure of her feelings…and he of his, that he'd stopped worrying and just let himself love her, and her him. Until that stopped, too.

His heart had long since mended, and the two of them had formed a fairly strong friendship that included a phone call every now and again, as well as contact via various social media sites. But that didn't mean he'd forgotten how much he'd once loved her or the pain that had followed.

Shaking off the bittersweet memories, he pulled into his parents' driveway and shut off the ignition. Jerry and Brenda Bradshaw lived in the center of Steamboat Springs, close to just about everything they'd want to be close to, in a one-level Craftsman-style house that they'd spent a considerable amount of time renovating. The prior owners hadn't had the money or skill to keep up on the maintenance, let alone the necessary updates. His parents, skilled in just about everything to do with home renovation, had done the bulk of the work themselves.

Naturally, they hired professionals for the wiring, plumbing and heating needs, along with repainting the house's exterior cornflower blue—his mother's favorite color—but within a year of moving in, their home was in tip-top shape inside and out.

And every Sunday, except when his parents were camping for the weekend or were out of town, was family day. Games. Dinner. Catching up. Nicole still lived in Denver, though she was also hoping to relocate to Steamboat Springs, but she visited about once a month. The Bradshaws had always been close. His sister's illness had made them even closer.

Nicole wasn't here this Sunday, but she would be next month for their mother's birthday. Thank the good Lord his sister was healthy and strong today, that she'd beaten the disease that everyone had been so afraid would take her life. And hell, yes, he'd been scared. But he also knew his sister, and he'd never stopped believing that she was strong enough to win her fight.

And she had.

Ryan pocketed his keys and stepped from the car, barely reaching the front porch when his mother swung open the front door with a huge, happy smile. You couldn't look at a smile like that and not feel good. Happy. But that was his mom. She had that way about her.

Her sunny attitude was as much a part of her as her blond hair and blue eyes, infectious laugh and generous heart. Nicole looked like her, while Ryan had his father's dark hair and eyes. But the positive outlook on life? Brenda had bestowed that precious gift on both of her children. Oh, he and his sister had also gained a fair share of their father's determination, his goal-oriented focus and, yes, his stubbornness. Good, solid traits that had helped more often than hurt. Yes, he and his sister had been blessed.

Another quality his mother possessed was the ability to never disappear in a crowded room, despite being barely five feet. Her presence was vivid and strong, much like his sister's. Hell. Much like Andi's, as far as that went. And he couldn't help but wonder if that quality was part of what drew his interest, which then led to more curiosity about the woman she had been before witnessing what she had, before being shot.

The woman he had no doubt still existed.

Damn. He yearned to know her, then and now. Since he couldn't slip into the past to introduce himself to an earlier version of Andi, he had to let that one go. Easy enough. Mostly, he just felt damn fortunate to have met her at all, to have her in his world today.

Whatever that might mean in the short term or the long term.

"Ryan!" Brenda said, meeting him at the bottom of the front porch steps and instantly wrapping him in a tight hug that smelled like herbs and spices, with a little something sweet tossed in. Meaning, she'd just left the kitchen. "I'm so glad to see you, honey."

He squeezed her back and kissed the top of her head before releasing her. "Glad to see you, as always. Though, it's only been a week," he teased. "You can't have missed me too much."

"Always miss my kids when they're not here, but I'm fortunate that you're close by. I just hope…" She trailed off and shrugged. "I look forward to our Sundays."

"I miss seeing Nicole, too," Ryan said, aware of the bond his mother and sister shared. "She's waiting on the right job opening. It will happen eventually. Gotta have faith, Mom."

"Of course I have faith! It's more about her being there by herself. I worry, but that's what parents do." She smiled again just as brightly. "Someday, you'll understand that the want to shield your children from pain never goes away. Doesn't matter how old you get, either."

"I don't have to wait for someday, I understand that now."

Reaching up, she patted his cheek. "You understand the concept, not the reality. Until you have a child, it is impossible to fully grasp."

Ah. Recognizing how easily this could lead them into the "I want grandbabies" conversation they'd had more than once over the past year, Ryan switched topics by asking, "Where is Dad, by the way? In the kitchen, sneaking bites of whatever you made for dessert?"

"Nope. He knows better." Laughing, Brenda started toward the front door. "He's out back, once again trying to perfect one of his golf swings before Wednesday's game. Don't ask me which swing, because I don't know. But he says that once he does, he'll be unbeatable."

Golf. His dad's fourth, sometimes fifth—depending on how active his sweet tooth was at any given moment—reason for living, after his wife and kids.

"I'm not sure what he thinks he's going to perfect. He already plays a damn solid game." Not a surprise, though, when Jerry's focus, determination and stubbornness were taken into account. If his dad thought he could do better, he wouldn't stop until he'd achieved that goal. "Honestly, Mom, I don't know why you don't play. I think you'd be really good."

"I might be," she agreed, leading him into the wood-floored entryway, "but your dad needs something of his own. This is it. Playing golf with his buddies. We share plenty of other hobbies, and I have more than enough on my own. I certainly don't need to add another."

That was one of the many reasons his parents got along so damn well. They understood each other's needs. Ryan could only hope he found the same someday. A companion. Someone who understood him and whom he understood. A friend. A partner. A lover. A confidante. A woman who challenged him to always be the best he could.

Andrea Caputo? Possibly. But…probably not. That did not stop Ryan from wishing that they'd already established a friendship. If they had, he might give in to the sudden instinct to call her, invite her here for dinner. But they'd barely broken ground. Doing so would cause her to question his motives, might even jeopardize any forward momentum.

Perhaps next month, when Nicole visited, they'd have a stronger base and he could invite her to his mother's birthday. Perhaps.

For the moment, he'd enjoy the afternoon with his parents, the meal—lasagna and tomato bread, he'd wager, based on the scents emanating from the kitchen—and relax. Tomorrow, the next day and every day following would take care of itself. One way or another.

That was a lesson *he* had learned.

And tomorrow already held the promise of being

an excellent day, simply due to the fact that he would see Andi again. Maybe he'd even find another way to make her laugh.

Thick, fat clouds stretched across a sky that was more gray than blue, promising rain at some point in the next several hours. There might even be a thunderstorm, complete with lightning. Andi hoped not. The loud cracks of thunder would send her adrenaline pumping and her heart racing. A lovely, light downpour, however, might just help her take a long afternoon nap, something she was in dire need of.

In the past few weeks, she hadn't beaten her three-hour record of continuous sleep, and last night, she hadn't managed even that. This needed to change soon, because she knew that without the proper amount of rest, everything she had come to Steamboat Springs to accomplish wouldn't occur. So, yes, the sound of rain drumming against her bedroom windows—minus the ricocheting bursts of thunder from an actual storm—might have a soothing effect, which might lead into a long, delicious, nightmare-free nap.

Carefully stretching out her legs in front of her, she closed her eyes and tried to ignore the wash of weakness that had overtaken her. Oh, today's session with Ryan hadn't been any worse than last week's, but maybe she'd pushed herself too hard. Or maybe not hard enough. Who knew? For the moment, though, for whatever reason, she was in pain.

Her aunt had texted her, letting her know that she was running late. Paul and Margaret owned a restaurant, Foster's Pub and Grill, as well as a sporting goods shop here in town, where all of Andi's cousins were also part owners and worked. There was a meeting this morning that had apparently gone longer than expected. Margaret had promised in her text that she'd get there as soon as she could, but figured she'd be at least another hour.

And that was fine. Andi understood. If she'd felt comfortable enough driving herself, she'd already be back at the house, sequestered in her bedroom. Hoping for rain. Hoping for sleep. Hoping for…amnesia, really.

Or a round of immense good luck, that would propel her out of this stuck place. Close to three weeks since arriving in Steamboat Springs and nothing had really changed.

"Andi? You okay?" Ryan's voice, deep and reassuring, came through the fog. She forced her eyes open and saw him standing in front of her with an expression of concern. "I didn't expect to see you out here still. Your aunt is usually waiting when we're done."

"She's running late, is all, by an hour or so. But I'm fine and she's fine. Nothing here for you to worry about."

"Good." Glancing at his watch, he smiled *that* smile. The one that brought the butterflies to life. "I'm free for another forty-five minutes, was about to take a short walk, stretch the legs a little before my next client. Feel like joining me? We don't even have to talk. Promise."

Lord. She wanted to say yes. Desperately so, even. Which was why she ignored that want and said, "Thank you, but no. Think I'll just sit here and wait for my aunt. Have fun, though, and if you see a four-leaf clover, save it for me."

"What do you need a four-leaf clover for? Seems you have plenty of luck on your side," he said, sitting next to her instead of taking his damn walk. Lovely. Now she could *smell* him—a strangely intoxicating mix of soap and shampoo and something else, something a tad spicy she couldn't identify—and their thighs were touching. "You seem tired, Andi. Did I work you too hard? Or still having problems sleeping?"

She ignored the luck comment and the query about her sleep, but answered his other question. "A little fatigued, but that's normal. Nothing to worry about, Ryan."

"Maybe. Maybe not." Thankfully, he stood then, so she could breathe again. "Come on, up and at 'em. Let's take that walk. I promise you'll feel better for it, and besides, there's something I want to show you. Something I think, hope, you'll appreciate."

When asked like that, how could she say no? And, yeah, he'd raised her curiosity. "You never learned how to take no for an answer, did you, Mr. Bradshaw? But okay, you win."

"I typically do," he said in a good-old-boy sort of way.

He held out his hand to help her up, but she stood on her own. As she always had, as she always would. The muscles in her leg complained viciously, which she ignored. She could handle a walk, and in the long run she'd probably be better off for it. If nothing else, the exercise would tire her even more, making it easier to take that nap later she so yearned for.

"You can quit looking at me as if I'm about to keel over," she said, holding her chin high. "I'm fine, as I said. And I've agreed to your walk, so let's get started before my aunt shows."

"Oh, I'm not looking at you as if you're about to keel over," he said, gesturing toward the driveway. "I'm also not looking at the dark circles beneath your eyes, or how your entire body just trembled as you stood. I've noticed those, yes, but what I'm looking at…what I'm seeing right now is fire. In your hair. In your eyes. In your demeanor. And, now, in your cheeks."

"Better be careful then." She followed his purposefully slow and even pace down the driveway, and tried not to be annoyed by her appreciation of his awareness and her discomposure by the very same. "Fire tends to burn. Wouldn't want to see you get hurt."

"Is that a warning?"

"No, not really. Let's call it an observation." Glancing over her shoulder, she grinned to lighten her words. "Fire is hot. Hot things burn. Burns cause pain. Therefore, one would be intelligent to remain cautious around fire."

"Fair enough."

They continued their easy stride, not talking at all, as they left Ryan's property and took a right from his driveway. Since he did not live in a neighborhood, there wasn't a sidewalk, so they hugged the street near the curb. After a few minutes had passed, Andi was forced to admit that the calm, rhythmic movement seemed to be doing her some good. The throbbing in her leg decreased, the tension in her shoulders eased and a good deal of the smog in her brain cleared.

Damn him for being right, anyway.

She felt so much better than she had just a few minutes ago, but she kept that thought to herself. What was it about this guy that got to her so keenly? How was he able to look at her and see so much truth so freaking easily? Others couldn't. She'd made sure of that.

This man could, though. He'd proved that several times already.

Suddenly, Ryan came to a stop and pointed toward a narrow path that jutted into the woods on that side of the road. "What I want to show you is in there. The path is a little rocky, but I think you can manage it just fine, as it's a fairly straight shot. Feel up to it?"

No. "Of course I do. Lead on."

"Actually, I want you to go first. That way I can catch you if you trip or lose your balance. And don't take that the wrong way, Miss Independent. I brought you here. It's my job to ascertain your safety, that's all this is."

Shrugging, she stepped onto the path, using her cane for balance, and said, "Why would I think anything else? You'll have to guide me, though, since I have no idea where we're headed."

"Nah. We're not going that far in, and you'll know when to stop."

With those words, she trudged forward, her entire focus on *not* falling or losing her balance, because the idea of Ryan's arms closing in around her was a little too appealing. Oh, hell, who did she think she was fooling? A *lot* too appealing.

"Keep going, we're almost there," Ryan said from behind her, his voice encouraging. Confident. "You're doing great and, once there—if we have a few extra minutes—we can sit and relax a bit before heading back."

Good. While the pain had receded to a much more manageable level, her muscles were shaky, still too weak for her comfort—from the workout earlier, the walk now and a definite lack of healing, restorative sleep.

Maybe it was time to consider the sleeping pills her doctor had prescribed months ago…the same ones she'd refused to take thus far. That was partially due to a groundless fear that they'd keep her locked in one of her nightmares, unable to rouse herself, and partially due to old-fashioned stubbornness. Pills might supply a temporary solution, but they weren't the answer. They wouldn't fix anything over the long term.

Lost in thought as she was, and not paying nearly enough attention to the path, her shoe hit a rock and she came close to losing her footing. Before she did, before so much as a speck of panic set in, a pair of strong and able arms pulled her backward into an equally strong and able hold. For a few brief—too brief?—seconds, Andi's body was pressed firmly against Ryan's, and in that minuscule period, she did not feel discomfort or uneasy.

Rather, a sense of utmost safety existed…which made sense, but something else lurked there, too. Recognition? Maybe. As strange as that possibility was, maybe that.

"You're fine," Ryan whispered into her ear, his tenor reassuring and his breath warm against her skin. Both of which elicited a series of tingles that began at her neck and wove their way down all the way to her freaking ankles. Crazy, to feel that way. Absurd, too. "I got you, Andi. I'm not about to let you fall, darlin'. Not today, anyway."

"Thank you," she said. "And you're right. I am fine. You can let me go now."

He did, without delay. "We're almost there," he said, once he seemed certain of her ability to stand on her own. "See that bend in the path up ahead? Our destination is just beyond."

"Then let's get to it," she said, more under her breath than not. Damn it. The phantom pressure of his arms remained, as did the sensation of their bodies plastered against one another. "Unless we hurry, I'll pretty much have to turn around as soon as we get there, anyway. My aunt is likely to worry if I'm not waiting outside your place when she arrives."

"Of course. That isn't a problem." The tone of his voice told her, without doubt, that she'd made him smile. Why? How? Jeez, what could she possibly have said or done to amuse him enough to bring forth a smile? "If I know you at all," he continued, sounding annoyingly confident, "you'll appreciate what you're about to see. And whether you like the idea or not, I'm beginning to know who you are."

"Lies," she said, going for light and easy. "All lies."

They started the trek around the bend, but she kept her mouth shut against the remaining slew of rebuttals bopping to and fro in her brain. She was not his darling, that was number one. In fact, she wasn't *anyone's* darling. Number two? Ryan only knew what she'd let him see, which hadn't been a hell of a lot. Because no matter what he thought and despite that *way* of his, he could not read her mind. He did not *know* her. And… and…she probably wouldn't have tripped, even without his help.

Probably, she'd have caught herself in time. She did not need Ryan Bradshaw, or anyone for that matter, swooping in and lifting her backward in his arms as if she were a bird with a wounded wing. She was not. Oh, and why—

Her body and her thought processes came to an abrupt halt at the exact same instant. She blinked and stared at the view that had morphed into being. She closed her eyes, opened them and stared again. Certainly, she'd somehow crossed a mystical barrier and now stood in a completely different world, because she had never before seen anything quite so beautiful.

As she stood and stared, the hard, jagged edges of her nerves softened, the pain in her leg disappeared, and the weight—that damn, one-thousand-pound weight that had snuffed out all joy—became much more manageable. Simply by the sight in front of her.

Multicolored rocks and stones lined the edges of a small body of water—no more than twelve to fifteen feet in diameter—that sat beneath a glossy umbrella of leaves. Wildflowers in a variety of shades, from the purest white to the boldest blue to the deepest violet, grew in scattered bunches outside of and in between the so-smooth-they-gleamed rocky boundaries. The effect was a tranquil type of loveliness, straight from one of Andi's childhood fairy tales, that brought a smile to her lips and peace to her heart.

All of this—the water, the flowers, the stones and rocks, the green leafy canopy—was beautiful in its own right, without anything else being added to the mix. But what made this scene so very special, so otherworldly stunning and almost too perfect be real, were the wispy tendrils of steam that swirled upward from the water's gleaming surface into the patches of sunlight that had broken through the heavy branches of the thick-trunked trees. Within this speckled light, the twisting puffs of steam began to glitter, becoming almost iridescent with the luminous sparkle of the most brilliant, the most lustrous, the most precious gemstones—a breathtaking display of diamonds, rubies, emeralds and sapphires—creating the illusion of fantasy, of magic.

And, oh, was it a glorious sight to behold.

For the first time in over six months, serenity stomped out Andi's anxiety, and true, unabashed hope stirred within her soul. Not only did she see the beauty in front of her, but the pureness of what she saw resonated all the way through. She felt real…almost whole.

"What is this place?" she asked, her tone hushed as she walked forward. "I don't ever want to leave. I want to live here, right at this spot."

"I often feel the same. As to your question," Ryan said, moving to stand beside her, "what you're looking at is a hot spring. Not a large one, obviously, but with the flowers, the trees, the way the light brings the steam to life, I thought you'd appreciate the serenity that exists here. Do you feel it?"

"Yes. To my bones." Then, without thought or concern for what he might think, she took one small step to the side, toward him, so close their hips touched, and put her head on his shoulder. "Why aren't there a ton of people here, soaking in the sight? I'm shocked we're alone."

"I'm not sure." He reached for her and then stopped, as if having second thoughts. "The path shows that others come here, but I've yet to stumble upon another person, and I'm typically here once or twice a week. Luck, I guess."

"Must be. This is way better than a four-leaf clover." Acting on instinct, she put her hand in his. Dangerous? Oh, yes, but also…right. "Thank you, Ryan. For bringing me here, for sharing this magical place with me. I… Seriously, thank you so much."

"You're very welcome, Andi. I agree. There is magic here, of a sort." The sturdiness of Ryan's body next to hers, the feel of his hand capturing hers and the warmth of his shoulder under her cheek all seemed, in that moment, like another type of magic. Not that she would utter such nonsense aloud. "I'm glad you see what I see, feel what I feel, in this place. It's a start."

"A start to what?"

"Oh, just about anything and everything, I'd say." His jaw brushed the top of her head before he pulled away. She missed his nearness, the comfort his presence gave her, instantly. "We should head back now, right?"

"Yes," she said, her mind locked onto his words. *Just about anything and everything.* What did that mean? What had *he* meant? "Someday, I'd like to come back. Stay for a while, maybe bring a picnic lunch and a book."

A pillow and a blanket, too, so she could rest. Here, she was sure, she'd be able to sleep for hours on end without a solitary nightmare. How could she not?

"Public property, Andi. You can return whenever you want." He tipped her chin so she had no choice but to look straight into his eyes. Lord. Those eyes would be the end of her if she stared into them too hard, for too long. "I won't ask you to promise that you'll bring someone else with you, but please make sure someone knows where you are. Anyone. Me, your aunt, your uncle. Just someone. The path is uneven. I don't want you to get hurt."

She almost argued. Almost told him that she was an adult who did not need to share her whereabouts with anyone. And, while sweet, his concern for her well-being was unnecessary and unheeded. She was fine. She should have said all of those things, except when she opened her mouth to do so, she found she couldn't. His concern was genuine. His care, for whatever reason, seemed authentic. And this man wanted her safe. She couldn't argue.

"Of course," she said in as crisp a tone as possible. "I promise that I won't visit here without someone else knowing, and when I do, I'll be cautious to not reinjure myself."

Ryan nodded once, sharply, and in tandem, they started down the path. It took every bit of willpower not to turn around and stare at the magical, mystical scene one last time before they rounded the bend. There wasn't any need. She would be back. Soon, if she had her way.

By the time they emerged onto the street, she could almost believe she really had visited another world. A world where everything and anything was possible, just as Ryan had alluded. Driving in a car by herself? Yes. Sleeping through the night? Yes. Letting go of the past? Yes. Feeling safe and comfortable in her own skin? Oh, hell, yes.

Likely, that was what he had meant. Precisely that and nothing more, nothing to do with the chemistry that sparked whenever they were together, the chemistry she was almost positive that he felt, as well. If all went well, by September she'd have returned to Rhode Island to her job at the hospital, and she would probably never see or hear from Ryan Bradshaw again.

But okay, if she were to someday fall in love? The head-over-heels, forever, no-holds-barred, full-blown-partnership type of love? She'd choose a man who shared the same qualities as Ryan: compassionate, kind, intelligent, sexy and strong and...a man who could make her smile. Bring her to laughter. A man with eyes that seemed to see straight through her skull and know exactly the person she was, even though she kept most of herself hidden.

Yes. If she were to fall in love, she'd want—no, demand—a man exactly like Ryan.

Chapter Four

Music. Amusement rides. Carnival games. Food, from corn dogs to pizza to salt-and-vinegar French fries to shrimp-fried rice and egg rolls. Alcoholic and nonalcoholic beverages. Booths filled with a variety of wares, some handcrafted and others not. There were pie-eating contests, water-balloon fights, three-legged races, tug-of-war games, movies at twilight and a variety of other activities scheduled for the next two days and nights.

The annual Steamboat Springs Summerfest was in its full, glorious swing, and the weather had cooperated nicely with mild temperatures and clear, sunny skies. Residents and tourists alike were enjoying everything the festival had to offer: the sights, sounds, appetizing scents and the company of whomever they'd brought with them.

Everywhere the eye could see were people—couples, families, clusters of friends—laughing, smiling, talking with their neighbors and strangers. And this, right here, was one of the reasons Ryan loved living in Steamboat Springs so damn much. The greater percentage of folks were kind and sociable, happy to be a part of an actual community.

And it was why he knew—beyond the fact that the rest of the family lived here—that his sister would love making her home in Steamboat Springs, as well. She was a people person. Always had been. Well, to a certain extent. She wasn't that fond of sharing her inner self, thoughts, feelings or worries with others, much like another woman he knew. But she was always there for those who needed her. Nicole was a giver, through and through.

"What do you think so far?" he asked his sister, who was in town to celebrate their mother's birthday. And who—thank God—looked happy and healthy. Settled, too, with herself. "Lots of kids here you might teach one day."

Nicole tucked a strand of honey-blond hair behind her ear and smiled. "This is terrific. Feels like an old-fashioned county fair, an arts-and-crafts festival and a music jamboree all rolled into one. And…maybe I'll teach some of these kids someday, but that could take a while. As could moving here. Unless I want to change careers, which I really don't. I love what I do."

In Denver, his sister worked as an elementary school music teacher. A position that was rather scarce to begin with, as most schools only kept one or, at most, two on staff. With budget cuts, a lot of schools were eliminating the position. And in a smaller community such as Steamboat Springs, there were far fewer grade schools that could possibly have an opening than in Denver. In addition, the teachers here tended to stick until they retired.

"You could teach privately," Ryan said, following Nicole as she pushed her way through the crowd toward an artist who was drawing caricatures. "Stay with me or Mom and Dad while you get everything going. Or until something else came through. That's always an option."

"For one, I don't see you allowing Roscoe to roam around your perfect house," she said, speaking of her large—very large—dog of unknown origins. Ryan cringed at the thought of Roscoe and his perpetually muddy paws but kept his mouth shut. "Furthermore, I need health coverage. Good health coverage. You know that."

"There are options there, too." But, okay, not great ones. "Whatever you need, you know we'll support you the best we can. That's what we do, Nic."

"Yup. I know." She grabbed his hand and tugged hard. "Let's get a caricature of us drawn for Mom, as part of her birthday gift. She'll love it. We'll even get it framed."

Ryan chuckled. "Yeah, she would love it. Okay, I'm game."

There were already several people ahead of them in line, so they took their place and continued to chat. As they did, Ryan continued to watch the crowd, looking for a certain auburn-haired beauty. Oh, he had no real reason to believe Andrea would be here today, as she certainly hadn't said anything about the festival this past week. But he doubted her family would skip this event, and if any of them were here...then yes, it made perfect sense that they'd bring Andi along.

"Who are you looking for?" his too-astute sister asked, humor lighting her tone. "And don't tell me no one, because you've barely paid attention to my last three comments."

Drawing his sister in close for a quick hug, he said, "No one really. Mostly just people watching, seeing if I recognize anyone I can introduce you to. Mom's getting antsy for grandbabies, you know. Figured since you're the oldest, you're up to bat first."

Nicole wrinkled her nose. "Yeah, let me get right on that," she said in a teasing manner that sounded hollow to Ryan's ears. "I know. I'll just dial one-eight-hundred-baby. Mom will be a grandma in no time. Should I order a boy or a girl? Or maybe twins?"

"If you're considering twins, why not triplets?" he said in dry humor. He winked at his sister, playing along, but he didn't miss the glimmer of sadness in her gaze. Something brewed there just below the surface. Now wasn't the time for a deep conversation. He'd ask her later when they had privacy. "I mean, hey, if you give Mom three grandbabies all at once, I'm forever off the hook. So yeah, that would be great. Thanks! You're the best sister!"

"Uh-huh. She'll never let you off that particular hook."

They moved up in line by one, and for the moment his thoughts were fully on Nicole. On what might have her concerned or, hell, scared. "You're still healthy, right?" he asked, unable to silence the query but knowing that if she hesitated the slightest amount in her response, they'd be in the car and on their way to his house in a New York minute. "Nothing has changed there?"

"Nothing has changed there," she confirmed instantly, squeezing his hand. "One hundred percent healthy. I promise, Ry-Ry. I'd have already told you if that status quo had changed. I'm cancer free."

Relief, swift and complete, settled in and took hold.

So much relief he didn't even balk at the nickname she'd insisted on calling him since he was a baby. "Okay. Good."

"And," she said softly, doggedly, "I still want to know who you were looking for. Just give me a name. No details necessary, and I won't ask any other questions. Just a name."

"Persistent today, I see."

"Always. Is there any other way?"

"No," he said with a smile. "Not for us, there isn't."

"Okay then. So…?"

"Andrea." He didn't mind giving in. In fact, saying her name came as another type of relief. "But she goes by Andi. I don't know if she's here, but that's who I was looking for."

"If you tell me what she looks like, I can keep an eye out, too. Point out possibilities as I see them," Nicole said easily, without so much as a whiff of curiosity. "Andi, huh? Good name."

"Yup. And…nope. Nice try, though."

Sniffing, his sister shrugged. "Well, I'll meet her if she's here. You can't not introduce us without appearing rude. And if there is one trait you absolutely don't have, it's rudeness."

He was about to respond when, out of the corner of his eye, he glimpsed fire. *Andi.* Her hair, in the sunlight, really did hold the deepest, most magnificent, hottest shade of fire. Gorgeous was what it was, especially when combined with her fair—almost alabaster, but warmer—complexion. Her cousin Haley was energetically talking and gesturing beside her, while Haley's husband, Gavin, trailed behind with a somewhat bemused expression. And Andi?

Even from where he stood, he could see she looked tired.

By her slower, wobblier-than-normal gait. By her slumped shoulders. By her pointed-straight-in-front-of-her gaze. Ryan didn't have to stand close to her to know that those damn dark circles still surrounded her eyes. So, her sleep hadn't improved. Not that she'd admit such a thing to him, or, he supposed, to anyone. Too strong, too proud, too independent.

She could lean on him, if she chose to. If she trusted him enough. If she'd just step toward him a tiny, minuscule inch, he'd meet her the rest of the way. But she had to take that step on her own free will. He couldn't, wouldn't, push. So really, all he could do was wait. Keep showing her who he was. And…hope. Because, despite his best intentions, he was pretty damn certain that his heart had already gone too far to retreat. And if it hadn't?

Well, he still wouldn't retreat. He simply did not want to.

"Our turn!" Nicole said, once again grasping Ryan's arm. "Finally. After this, let's get some food. I'm starving and…" Her words disappeared into the air as she apparently noticed her brother's preoccupation. "Oh. Andi? Where is this mystery woman?" Standing on her tiptoes, Nicole stared in the direction of Ryan's gaze. "She's the redhead in the purple T-shirt, isn't she?"

"Yes. How'd you figure that out so ridiculously fast?"

"I don't know. Call it women's intuition."

"How about spooky? Let's go with that." Then, forcing his gaze away from Andi, who'd yet to notice his or Nicole's stares, thank goodness, he nodded toward the several empty stools in front of the caricature artist. "I think we're holding up the line. Ready to do this?"

Nodding, his sister moved forward, sat down and patted the stool next to her, not saying another word about Andi or Ryan's obvious interest. She was good that way, his sister. Nicole wouldn't directly mention the topic again unless he did. Okay, she might if something were to occur that concerned her enough to question Ryan, but that was to be expected. And he appreciated both her reticence and that she loved him enough to butt in if she deemed it necessary.

"Okay, you two, strike a pose," said the artist, a middle-aged man wearing Harry Potter type glasses and a black fedora hat. "Are you two married or...?"

"Oh, no! We're brother and sister, not a couple," Nicole said, leaning closer to Ryan. "And this drawing will be a gift for our mother's birthday."

"Got it," the artist said. "Ready?"

Tucking one arm around his sister's shoulders and giving her rabbit ears with his other hand, Ryan nodded that they were, indeed, ready.

"Perfect." Without delay, the artist's hand almost flew across the oversize paper clipped to the easel. "Just keep smiling. This won't hurt at all."

No, having a silly drawing made of his and Nicole's likenesses wouldn't hurt, but giving his heart to Andi certainly could and probably would cause some pain. Better, though, to risk that potential fallout than to give up without trying. Ryan did not—never had, never would—tackle anything by half, and if he walked away now, he'd forever wonder about what might have been.

He supposed that was yet another lesson he'd learned: what-ifs were the devil and should be avoided at all cost.

* * *

A telltale tingle, along with those annoying butterflies, had informed Andi that Ryan was somewhere nearby, likely watching her. But she purposely did not turn her head to seek him out. If incorrect in her hunch, she didn't want to know if she'd feel disappointment. And if, on the other hand, her instincts had proved correct, good manners would dictate, at the very least, a greeting and some general conversation.

Neither would present a problem under normal circumstances, but ever since Ryan had taken her to that fantastical, magical hot spring near his house, nothing between them resonated as normal. Somehow, she had connected that moment of peace to *him*. And she'd caught herself yearning for more…thinking about more and considering possibilities that weren't in any tangible way possibilities at all. For all the reasons she'd already analyzed.

So, she stuck to her guns and did not search for those solid, firm shoulders, sinfully dark brown eyes or that smile she so loved. She just kept walking, listening as Haley talked about the camp for foster kids that she and her husband ran, and how it would come in really handy to have a nurse on staff whenever camp was in session. Andi wasn't stupid. Her cousin was trying to offer her a choice so that, if she didn't want to return to Rhode Island or her prior job, she could stay here and work for Gavin and Haley.

Nice, sure. Generous and considerate? That, too. But Andi didn't believe her cousin was serious as much as she was verbally speculating, and even if she was… well, her true goal was to work in a hospital again. Before the shooting, Andi had absolutely loved her job at

Juliana Memorial and almost everything about it, including the hectic nature.

Fortunately, Haley hadn't pushed the topic, and after a minor amount of grumbling from Gavin, they'd decided to take a break from their wandering. Now they were enjoying a meal in an enclosed area where a local band was setting up to play. Andrea had already decided that once they were done eating, she'd sit here for a while and let Gavin and Haley peruse more of the festival without her slowing them down. They could enjoy some alone time while she continued to rest and ponder her current situation.

Her biggest issue by far was her inability to sleep. Either she was too afraid of facing another nightmare to fall asleep easily or one of those very same nightmares awakened her, filling her with fear and nervous energy that kept her eyes wide open through sunrise. And then the new day began.

She could not keep this up for much longer. Eventually her body would collapse and she'd end up back in the hospital, where they would drug her to insure she received the necessary sleep. Again, though, a temporary solution that wouldn't solve the core problem.

Obviously, she hadn't reconciled what she had witnessed and gone through on that December afternoon. Until she did, she would continue to have nightmares as her brain processed what couldn't be changed. Yet, for her body and mind to fully heal, she needed to freaking sleep. It seemed like a vicious cycle with no path out, but there had to be a way.

Sighing, she stabbed her fork into her pasta salad and took a bite. Damn it, she had really hoped that coming to Steamboat Springs would offer her enough differences from life at home that she'd find her way. Almost a full month later and that hadn't happened. Okay then, this problem could not be solved by a simple change in location. The solution lurked inside of her, somewhere.

She just had to find it.

"You're very quiet over there, Andi," Haley said, obvious concern echoing in her words. "Everything okay?"

"Yes!" Andi forced cheer into her response and smiled. "Everything couldn't be better! I'm glad you insisted I come with you two this morning. In fact, I was quiet because I was thinking about how I need to visit more of those art booths and try to find a painting of the mountains to take home. It would be nice to have a visual remembrance of being here."

Also, when she next visited the hot spring, she planned on photographing the scene and then later having the shots blown up and framed. She'd hang the pictures on her bedroom walls so she'd never forget the beauty or the serenity or the magic. Or, for that matter, the connection she'd experienced so vividly with Ryan in that place, on that day. Her cheek on his shoulder, their hands entwined and that feeling of…rightness that had enveloped her.

"I'm fairly sure we'll be able to find the perfect mountain-scene painting. They're everywhere. Literally, everywhere," Haley said with a grin that lit up her green eyes. "And we'd already decided before surprising you this morning that you were coming with us. One way or the other. You didn't really have a choice."

"Oh, I didn't, did I?"

"Nope. So it's good you didn't argue!"

Quiet resumed for a few minutes, and then Gavin

asked, "How are you feeling? We're not wearing you out, are we? I have no idea what it's like to recover from bullet wounds and surgeries, let alone anything you witnessed, but I imagine you tire easily."

"I'm fine. A little tired, definitely, but it's manageable." *No.* She couldn't think about what she'd witnessed. Not now and not here. And she certainly couldn't discuss anything to do with that topic—including her recovery— either, but she sensed the conversation was heading in that direction. *Don't panic.* What was it Ryan had said? Oh. Keep it simple. "And no, not easy, but I'm feeling stronger every day that passes. It's just…a process."

"Yup. Most challenges are," Gavin said. "But I'm glad to hear you're stronger. Coming back from that type of an experience can't be easy. I'm—" he ran his hand over his short, trimmed beard, looking a tad self-conscious "—sorry you've gone through what you have. Wish you hadn't."

"Nothing for you to be sorry for, but I appreciate the sentiment."

"We're all sorry, Andi," Haley said, her voice filled with compassion. "We were scared when we first heard the news reports. Mom couldn't get a hold of your mom right away, so we didn't know if you were working that day, if you were there. If you were all right." She blinked, glanced down at her hands. "I stalked your Facebook page until we knew you were… *Okay* isn't the right word. Safe, I guess. On your way to being okay."

"She did," Gavin confirmed. "I couldn't drag her so much as an inch from her tablet. I worried, too, even though I didn't know you. Haley loves you, that was all that mattered. I didn't need to personally know you to hope you were okay."

Tears gathered and burned but didn't fall at these startling words from Haley and Gavin. Why startling? They shouldn't be. She'd have felt the same, would've done the same, if the situations were reversed. Somehow, though, hearing of what had taken place here while she battled everything she had there just…stunned her. Reminded her of her value at a time she didn't often feel so valuable. Hard to believe in yourself when so much of the person you used to be had seemingly vanished, seemingly never to return.

"Thank you," she whispered. It was all the volume she could muster. "For telling me, for caring then and for caring now. It's been tough, trying to put the pieces back together, but I think, slowly but surely, it's starting to happen."

"Good," Gavin said. "From my view—for what that's worth—you've made incredible strides. It's impressive and you should be proud of yourself."

"Ah. Well, I still have a ways to go." Absently, Andi rubbed her denim-covered leg, thinking of the scars that she'd always have. Physically, emotionally. And wondering how many more miles she'd have to tread. "Quite a ways, actually. But yes, my leg is healing, growing stronger, every day. I'm beginning to think Ryan's torture methods are paying off, and—"

"Torture methods?" Ryan's voice slid over her like warm water as he stepped into view. "Really, Andi? I'm hurt, but I suppose if you think they're paying off, you can call them whatever you like. Wish you'd chosen a different word than torture, though. Maybe something along the lines of, 'Wow, Ryan's methods are amazing! He's a miracle worker!'"

Heat spread from Andi's cheeks to her neck and then

downward another several inches. "Miracle worker? You've got to be kidding me," she said, deciding her best bet was to keep the joke going. "Torturous is the perfect description. Why, most days I feel lucky I don't need a wheelchair to get to the car. Or a gurney. Or—"

"Why, darlin', you don't need a wheelchair or a gurney. I'm more than happy to pick you up and carry you to the car." Ryan winked and, yep, there was that smile. God, she loved that smile. Even if she shouldn't. "Just say the word."

"Uh-huh, I'm sure that will happen soon." This came from a new voice. A female voice that, once she slipped into place beside Ryan, Andi could see belonged to a lovely blonde cherub with huge blue eyes. "You men, always thinking we women want to be carted off somewhere. Trust me, we don't! And hi, everyone. I'm Nicole, Ryan's older and savvier sister."

Ah. *Sister.* Andi wouldn't have guessed siblings based on the wide disparity in their coloring—Ryan's dark hair and eyes versus Nicole's blond hair and blue eyes—but okay, now that she knew, there were similarities. Faint, but there. In the shape of their eyes, the cadence of their speech, maybe even in the way they held their bodies.

And, dang it all, a rush of relief that this sweet, fairly beautiful woman was Ryan's sister and not his date or his girlfriend solidly hit Andi over the head. Silly, of course, but there it was. She didn't bother denying the relief. There wasn't any use in kidding herself.

"Hi, Nicole. I'm Andi, and this is—" Andi gestured to the other side of the table "—my cousin Haley and her husband, Gavin." Should she invite Ryan and Nicole to join them? Probably. It would seem odd not to. "We're taking a much-needed sustenance break after traipsing around for the past several hours. You're welcome to join us, if you'd like?"

"Oh, yes!" Haley said. "Please do."

"We'd love to," Nicole said. She nudged her brother. "Wouldn't we, Ry-Ry?"

"Ry-Ry? Seriously?" A laugh escaped as Andi glanced from Nicole to Ryan. "I am so calling you that from now on. As often as I can get away with it. Because that's a precious nickname and makes me think of a cuddly, purring kitten. Cuddly kittens can't inflict torture!"

Ryan's brow arched and he grimaced. "Great. Just what I want to be compared to. A vibrating mop of fur. But yes," he said, "we'd love to join you. Thanks for the invite."

Nicole set down her plate on one side of Andi, while Ryan took the other side, and for the next little while, everyone focused on their food. Well, Andi pretended to eat. Truth be told, she was finding it rather difficult to swallow, so after a few minuscule bites, she gave up. She hadn't wanted to see Ryan earlier, but now that he sat next to her, she also couldn't deny the warm glow that suddenly infused her heart. Hell. She wouldn't be altogether surprised if her entire body radiated from it, for all the world to see.

For everyone at this table to see.

"You don't really think of our sessions as torture, do you?" Ryan asked quietly from her left. "If so, that's something I should know. Discomfort is one thing, but if you're in serious pain, we should consider scaling back some."

"I was joking."

"Are you sure? Because, quite honestly, Andi, you're

looking more and more exhausted every time I see you. If it's the—"

"It's not that."

"Then what is it?"

"Lack of sleep," she said in a near whisper, surprising herself at the admittance. "Please don't ask for details, as I won't talk about the reasons why, but I'm not getting nearly enough sleep. You were right on that front, and it's a problem I'm working on. I know I need to figure it out, Ryan. And I will. You don't need to worry."

Eyes narrowed in contemplation, Ryan nodded. "The only problem I have in everything you just said is the continuous use of the word 'I.' You're not alone in this. If you let me in on what's interrupting your ability to sleep, I might be able to help. *We* might be able to find a solution together. Because you're right, this needs figuring out. Posthaste."

"I don't do 'we' that well." And she didn't. But the idea appealed. More than it should. "I do appreciate the offer, though, and I'll keep it in mind. That is the best I can do right now."

He didn't say anything in response, just nodded and ate some of his lunch. He laughed when his sister showed off the caricature they'd had drawn for their mother's birthday and answered a few general questions about his career, when Haley asked. And when he discovered that Gavin had also grown up in Denver, he asked a few questions of his own.

As the conversation around the table continued, Andi's defenses relaxed and she added her opinion here, a laugh at a joke there and, for the most part, genuinely enjoyed herself. But she didn't doubt that at some point, likely soon, Ryan would revisit the topic of "we," and when he did, she'd have to remain strong. Outside of her physical rehabilitation, they were not a "we."

Regardless of how *appealing* the concept, she wouldn't take so much as one step down that path. Because if she did, she'd only be asking for heartache later. She needed to rely on herself, not on anyone else. Not even a man who made her feel alive, whose presence seemed to send her shadows scurrying for cover. Someday wasn't today. She wasn't ready for "we."

Not even with a man like Ryan Bradshaw.

Chapter Five

Had he ever met such a stubborn woman? Well, yes. His mother and sister came to mind, but with them, Ryan could usually maneuver past whatever wall they'd built. Andi's walls were thicker, denser and—at least from where he stood—immovable. Oh, he had every intention of gaining traction, of breaking that particular wall into smithereens so she'd open up about her sleep issues… He just had to decide how.

And if he couldn't, then he'd find someone who could. It didn't take a rocket scientist, a doctor or, hell, a physical therapist to see that Andrea couldn't continue this way much longer. Up close, her dark circles were a blackish purple, her already pale skin almost had a translucent quality, and any amount of physical strain seemed to send a series of trembles through her body. He didn't like to see her this way so, yeah, he was worried.

About Andrea Caputo, his client whose well-being was important to him for professional reasons, *and* about Andi, the woman he already cared for deeply, perhaps *too* deeply.

The fact she'd shared even as much as she had about

her inability to sleep unequivocally showed that progress had been made. She'd opened up to him, hadn't she? It did not matter how little information she'd chosen to share—she *had* shared. The next step was his. A step he planned on taking right this very instant.

Gavin, Haley and his sister had finished eating and, as a trio—with a little prodding from Ryan—had taken off to check out more of the festival, leaving him and Andi alone. She'd stated her plan to stick around, listen to the band and relax more before searching for the "perfect" mountain-scene painting, and when he said he'd do the same, help her find said painting when she was ready, he could see she wanted to argue. But she hadn't.

So, here they were. Alone in a public, social setting instead of a professional one. Hell, yes, he was taking that next step before Haley, Gavin and Nicole decided to return.

"Come on," he said to Andi as he stood and held his hand toward her. "It's time."

She narrowed her eyes. "Time for what, exactly?"

"Dancing," he said. "Didn't think I'd forgotten my promise, did you?"

"Oh." With a vigorous head shake, she said, "I'm okay with you breaking that promise."

"Now come on, Andi, that's a slippery slope," he teased. "Why, you let me break one promise, and soon enough, I'll be breaking all of my promises. No one will trust me then. I'll lose my family, friends and possibly even my career. I'll end up destitute, living on the streets, wondering where it all went wrong. You can't let that happen to me!"

"Exaggerate much?" A light, quirky grin appeared.

"Besides which, your promise was about showing me your drunken-elephant-on-ice dance. I'm certainly not stopping you from that performance. In fact, I can't wait to see it."

"Ah, no. Your memory, darlin', is failing you. I promised I would *take you dancing*, with the added bonus of witnessing my lack of skill on the dance floor." He grinned. "I have a very clear recollection on the promise itself. You can't talk your way out of this one, Andi."

One blink. Two blinks. And then a sharp nod. "Okay. You win. But only for a single song, and then I'm done." Insecurity, doubt, flooded her features. "If I even can dance, that is."

"You definitely can. Let me show you."

Still she hesitated, but not for long. A few seconds at most passed before that stubborn gleam hit her eyes, and she nodded again. Carefully, she pushed out of her chair and stood, reached for his hand and, ignoring her cane, allowed him to lead her to the center of the enclosed area. To the dance floor, where there were already several people dancing. "I'm nervous," she admitted in a low, barely audible voice. "I don't want to fall."

"I won't let you fall." Whether it was fate or coincidence or something else entirely, he couldn't say, but the band finished their upbeat song and moved onto a slower one, a song meant for couples. And finally, he pulled this woman he worried about, thought about, wondered about…dreamed of, into his arms. "Trust me on that, if nothing else. You will not fall with me."

"Okay. I won't fall," she said, looking into his eyes. "Because you won't let me."

"That's right." It took all the strength he could muster not to make her other promises. Such as, she'd never have to fight any battle alone, ever again. That he'd fight right alongside her, offering her his strength, his support when she needed it. As a friend or maybe, someday, as more. Maybe. Hopefully. But hell, friendship was good. "Dance with me, beautiful."

She rested her head against his shoulder, encircled his waist with her arms, and together they found the soft, sweet rhythm of the love song that was playing and they started to move. Her hair smelled like summer—coconuts and lime and flowers—and, Lord, her body fit well with his or, he supposed, his body fit well with hers. Either way, both ways, they just worked.

"Talk to me," he said. "While we dance."

"About what?"

"Anything. Your favorite movie, your best and worst childhood memory, if you ever played sports as a kid, what makes you laugh, what makes you sad or…maybe, you might be able to let me in on why you can't sleep." *Talk to me, beautiful. I'm right here.* "Anything at all."

"I don't have a favorite movie. I have many," she said without missing a beat. "My best childhood memory is when I learned how to ride a horse. My dad taught me, and we had the greatest day. My worst? Hmm. I don't know, really. My childhood was pretty great."

So, Andi could ride a horse. Learning to do so was her favorite memory, even. This knowledge gave Ryan an idea. Not for now, but for some time in the coming weeks. He'd take her horseback riding, help her remember that day with her dad and show her how far she'd come, physically, since the shooting. "Thank you for sharing," he said. "Keep going. Tell me more."

He couldn't see her face, but he'd bet money she'd just wrinkled her nose at his request. "No, to the sports question," she said with an elongated sigh. She didn't lift her head from his shoulder, though, and he interpreted that as a very good sign. "I wasn't much into sports as a kid, other than riding horses and swimming. I read a lot of books, listened to a lot of music, spent hours on the phone with my friends. I was the average girl, doing the normal type of girl stuff."

"Nothing about you is normal, Andrea. Or average," he said quietly. "But don't misunderstand those comments. I mean them in all the best ways. You're warm and giving, sweet and—when the mood strikes—funny. You're also intelligent, stronger than you think, very focused and…well, perhaps a mite too independent. I'm working on that, though."

"I've always been that way," she admitted. "It's smarter to rely on your own capabilities than expect other people to save the day or pick up the slack or whatever. But thank you for seeing me as intelligent and giving and funny, and everything else you said."

"You're welcome. Now, about your sleep?"

"It's… I haven't told anyone, Ryan," she said, lifting her head to look once again into his eyes. She hadn't even told the therapist she saw for a few months, right after the shooting. "So please understand, my unwillingness to give detail isn't restricted to you. Again, this is who I am. Given some more time, I'm sure to figure it out."

The song ended, but there were a good number of couples on the dance floor, so the band wisely chose to play another slow melody. Thank God. Ryan wasn't ready to stop holding Andi.

"How about we try it this way?" he asked, following his instincts. *All* of his instincts. "I'll ask you a question, and you let me know if I'm right or wrong. If I'm right, I'll ask a few more questions. That way, you might not have to say much more than yes or no. Can we try that?"

He thought he'd pushed too hard, based on the tension that rolled through her body—which he easily felt—and her sharp intake of breath, but then she showed her bravery…her desire to *try*, and she said, "I guess we can give it a go, but no promises. I'll see how each question feels."

Closing his eyes for a millisecond, Ryan inhaled deeply. He hadn't anticipated her agreement. His goal had been to give her yet another reminder that he was on her side, her team, and nothing more. But she had agreed. She'd given him an opening. Perhaps the start of dismantling this particular wall. If he proceeded with caution. If he didn't push too hard.

He was also—whether he should or should not be—proud of Andi.

"I'm thinking there are three possible causes to your sleep problem," he said, holding her close so she couldn't bolt. Also, he just liked holding her close. So there was that. "One of which is that your brain won't stop processing when you finally get in bed. You think about the day, a conversation you had, the shooting—whatever, from small to large—and your brain keeps cycling through, refusing to stop long enough for you to relax enough to actually fall asleep. Does this happen to you?"

"Yes. But…that's not the entire issue."

Yup, and that was not unexpected. She'd identified one area he might be able to help her with, though. "I'm sorry," he said. "I've faced that particular issue before.

When the mind won't rest, the body finds it almost impossible to do the same."

"Yes," she repeated. "I've found that to be true."

He waited close to a minute before speaking again, in case she chose to add information to that which she'd already supplied, but she remained silent. *Okay then, moving on.* "When we're asleep, we become vulnerable. Not only to outside forces, but internally, as well. If there is something we're struggling with during our awake hours, this struggle might show itself in a dream. Or a nightmare. And these dreams are often repetitive, which—"

He broke off as she stopped dancing and her entire body hardened within his hold, muscle by muscle. She could've turned into a solid stone statue, she became so unmoving. Hell, he didn't even think she was breathing. By this response, Andi's dark circles and perpetual exhaustion, he knew he'd found the issue: nightmares. The core issue, of course, was whatever caused the nightmares, but knowing this much gave him a starting point.

"Nightmares, huh?" he asked. "Every single night?"

"Like clockwork, yes. I'm…usually awake after about three hours, sometimes less. And when I wake up, I'm panicked," she said. "Which then makes it difficult to fall back to sleep. I usually just watch television, drink some tea, until the sun rises."

Three hours. "Ouch. No wonder you're exhausted." The question that should be asked, that just about begged to be asked, was in reference to the nightmares themselves. He could guess what they were about—the shooting, what she'd seen and experienced—but did the nightmares alter, or were they always of one specific moment? It was an important question, but not one he thought she would answer. Not yet, anyway. Instead, he said, "I'm so sorry. I wish there was a way I could gift you with a solid eight hours. I'd pay any amount of money."

"Me, too."

"Hey," he said. "I get that you're not prepared to share everything with me. Just do me a favor and consider talking about the subject of these nightmares with *someone*. I can recommend some counselors, or if that doesn't appeal to you, maybe your aunt. Or a friend back home you can call. Haley. Just someone, Andi. Simply talking about it might help."

"I saw a therapist for a while, but maybe I wasn't ready. I don't know, but yes, I'll think about talking to someone."

"Do that." To alleviate Andi's discomfort, he chose to change the topic. "We've danced through two songs now, and you're holding up just fine. Told you that you could dance."

"This? You can't call this dancing, Ry-Ry," she said, her tone lighter. Slightly sarcastic, too, which he appreciated. "I'm leaning on you and shuffling my feet. Barely, at that."

"It counts, but…" Trailing off, Ryan waited as the current slow song came to an end, guessing the band would choose a fast, get-on-the-floor-and-dance tune next. And yes, "Footloose" fit the bill. Almost perfectly, to Ryan's frame of mind. "There we go. Let's give this a shot."

"Oh," she said, stepping out of his embrace. A sad state of affairs, but necessary. "How about if I take a seat and watch you in action? I've already done my part and danced, right? I mean, you said so yourself."

"Whatever you want, Andi," he said easily, his goal to remind her that she was in control. "If you'd rather just watch, that's fine by me."

Indecision flickered, as plain as day, proving that what he guessed to be true was the case. She wanted to dance, was either worried she couldn't or felt self-conscious. Or a bit of both. But this, like so many other areas, had to be her choice. *She* had to decide if she was willing to slough off her concerns and her fears for a chance at a little fun. And yeah, he probably could—based on her indecision—talk her into taking the risk. But even if he was right on that, doing so wouldn't be fair. For Andi. Maybe for him, too.

"I don't know. Let me think." Putting more weight on her right leg than her left, as if testing its stability, she breathed in and, a heartbeat later, nodded. "Okay. I guess I would like to try. But only for one song. You can dance like a fool and I'll work on keeping my balance."

Proud of her decision, her bravery, he shrugged as if he hadn't been waiting on tenterhooks. "Great!" he said. "The song is halfway over now, though, so how about we try for one more after this? Then, assuming you still want to and can summon the energy, we'll scour the entire festival until we find your perfect painting. Or, if not that, something else."

A rush of emotion roared into existence at Ryan's words, his quiet way of being there, of offering support without stripping her of her independence. Yet another quality Andi valued. Add that to the rest, and this man was becoming extraordinarily hard to resist. But she did not have to worry about her *crush* right now, not when he was waiting for her to dance. Not when she wanted to prove to herself that she could.

She closed her eyes and let the music surround her, let it soar into her ears and through her body, until muscle memory kicked in and every part of her itched with the urge to move. *Now* she was ready. Opening her eyes, she smiled at Ryan—a true, to-her-gut sort of smile— and stopped thinking. Stopped worrying. Stopped being self-conscious and just…danced.

Her body felt freer, more fluid, than it had in close to seven months. Oh, she had to be careful not to put too much pressure on her right leg, but she also found herself stronger, more agile, than she'd believed. She didn't have to baby her leg, which came as a huge and delightful surprise. And the longer she danced, her joy at being here with Ryan increased in bursting gulps.

It was then, however, that she noticed Ryan had not moved so much as an inch. He looked frozen, his gaze intent and focused on her, a smile lifting the corners of his lips. And, yes, she loved his smile, even enjoyed the directness of his attention, but…he was supposed to be showing off his drunken elephant dance steps. And he was not.

Dancing closer to him, she said, "You don't resemble an elephant to me, Ry-Ry. Not in any way at all. You're not even moving! Are you having second thoughts? Because if so, I'll have you know how unfair that is, since I'm—"

That was all she managed to say before his arms swooped around her and he dragged her to him. "You have no idea how beautiful you are, do you, Andi?" he said, his mouth at her ear, his breath warm, sending a sheath of shivery goose bumps down the back of her neck. "Or how crazy I am about you. Or how difficult it is to remember I'm your physical therapist. Or how much I no longer care about dancing. All I want is to…kiss you."

Wait…what? "You're crazy about me? You want to…"

"Yes, Andi. I'm crazy about you *and* I want to kiss you."

Oh, this was bad. In the "trouble is knocking, are you going to answer?" sort of way, and not due to what he'd said. Or even that he wanted to kiss her. Because, okay, that thought—the mere image of Ryan's lips on hers and hers on his—brought every one of her senses to life. The colors around her became brighter, more vivid. The music, the rumble of people talking and laughing, even the sound of her breathing grew in strength and clarity. And the scents floating in the air—food being the most prevalent, but Andi recognized the smell of suntan lotion, perfume and fresh-cut grass, to name a few, lingering beneath—multiplied in intensity by four.

If those three senses had magnified, what would their lips touching…tasting him for the first time ever…do to her? Oh, yeah, this was bad. But it was also too glorifying a possibility to ignore. To resist or to walk away from.

And there were plenty of other physical therapists in Steamboat Springs. Ryan did not have to be hers.

No doubt about it, regrets were sure to consume her later, but she heard herself saying, "I'm standing right here, Ryan." She flipped her hair over her shoulder and met his direct gaze with her unflinching one. "If you want to kiss me, then I think that is what you should do."

Heat unfurled in her stomach and the myriad of scents, mash of sounds and vivid colors all around her faded into nonexistence. All she saw, all she felt, was Ryan.

"Are you sure, Andi? This complicates everything,"

he said, his voice a rough melody of need and hope. Desire and, yes, longing, too. Everything she felt resonated in his words. "We couldn't work together, and you should know I'm not playing a game. I don't randomly kiss women for the sport of it. So, darlin', as much as I hate to say this, if you're not ready for anything other than a kiss, we shouldn't start on this path."

"I don't know what path you're referring to," she said, backing out of his arms. "A kiss doesn't have to mean anything other than what it is. And…and…"

"And?"

He was being honest with her. She needed to do the same, for both of their sakes. And, yes, the honest truth was, "No. I'm not ready." Blinking, she dipped her chin so he couldn't wield his Ryan voodoo and see into her brain, read her thoughts. Her disappointment. "I guess I got carried away in the moment. I'm sorry."

Fifteen seconds, maybe, passed before he said, "Hey."

"Is for horses?"

"Yup. But also, there isn't a thing in the world for you to be sorry for, though you might feel different in…oh, about twenty seconds. Give or take. And," he said with the faintest spark of humor, "you might want to back up a little more. I need a decent amount of space, you see, in order to really show off my skills."

What? Those few words, delivered in Ryan's light and relaxed tempo, dissolved the heat of the moment and the greater amount of Andi's discomfort. Confused, she lifted her head while taking two large steps backward, and then she almost fell over from the burst of laughter that all but roared from her chest. Oh, dear. No. This man *seemingly* could not dance.

He moved his entire body in a swaying motion, side

to side and then forward and backward, which wouldn't be bad all on its own. But he kept his head and shoulders angled downward so he stared at the floor, and every few seconds he'd sort of rear his entire upper torso backward and up, stare at the ceiling and then return to his prior position.

She swallowed another gulp of laughter when he shimmied to the side, waved his head to and fro, and shimmied back the other way. Oh, good grief. Yes, his sister was correct. Drunken elephant on ice definitely fit the bill, but…she didn't buy any of it. Not one little bit.

Nobody—man, woman or child—could naturally dance this poorly. No, what she was seeing was a carefully orchestrated performance, likely one he'd perfected over the years, to—knowing Ryan—make people laugh, so they'd relax and focus on him instead of themselves. It was, she decided, definite Ryan-type behavior. He thought of others far more often than he thought of himself. She'd guessed that early on, but this ridiculous and heartwarming and hilarious and sweet—so freaking sweet—display made her like him even more.

He'd almost kissed her. If she'd been brave enough, strong enough, all she would have had to say was, *Yes, I'm ready. Kiss me, Ryan.* Except that would've been a lie. Or maybe just wishful thinking. Regardless, she wasn't ready. Not yet, anyhow.

But she had a lot of thinking to do, about the work still in front of her and where Ryan fit. As her partner in recovery or as something different. Something more. Maybe something much more?

It was possible. And if so, she only had a few short months to get herself ready for all that could, likely would, entail.

* * *

Several hours after the crazed elephant dance and one lovely painting of the Rocky Mountains later, which Andi had purchased on the spot, they were walking the outer edge of the festival, lazily looking for their lost family members. Andi had texted Haley a full thirty minutes earlier but had yet to receive a response. The same went for Ryan texting Nicole.

So, they had decided to take another stroll around and through the festival grounds, hoping to catch sight of the rest of their group. No luck so far, but there were a lot of people to scan through. As the afternoon became early evening, it seemed the attendance had doubled. The rest of Steamboat Springs had to feel abandoned, there were so many folks here. And while she was tired, her leg throbbing and a headache brewing at her temples, Andi wasn't ready to call it day. She should. But doing so would mean saying good-night to Ryan.

And for that reason alone, she wasn't searching all that hard for Haley, Gavin and Nicole. They'd run across them soon enough without her speeding the process any.

"I'm so on to you," she said to Ryan, referring to his supposed lack of dancing skill. It had taken her this long to decide to say anything at all. "But you made me laugh, and I stopped feeling self-conscious. So, thank you. Even if you broke my heart with your lies."

"What lies?" He tossed her a grin. "So far as I know, I've never outright lied to you."

"And that makes lie number two!"

He shrugged in a clueless manner, saying, "I've always danced like that. Just ask Nicole. Or, actually, ask my parents. Tomorrow is my mother's birthday. You could always join us."

"For your mother's birthday? That's a family celebration."

"So was the barbecue at your aunt and uncle's," he pointed out. "Not a huge difference."

"Well, yeah, but...oh, no you don't. Stop trying to change the subject!"

Facing her, he said, "Okay. You're partially right. A few years back I took a couple of classes, so now, if I put forth the proper amount of effort, I can manage to not look quite so foolish. That being said, without the classes or the effort, what you saw is my...ah...natural style. I wasn't lying to you. I simply neglected to mention the entire story."

"Right. You lied by omission," she said, shaking her head pitifully. "My heart is truly breaking. I never thought you were capable of such deceit!"

"Overplaying your hand a bit, aren't you?" He gently tugged her hair as if she were his sister, and she tried not to let that bother her. "My entire goal was to see you happy. So you'd smile and have fun. I wanted you to feel alive. Nothing wrong with that, in my book."

And there he went again, being sweet and charming and melting her heart with his words. "What am I going to do with you, Ryan?" she asked. "I hope you have an answer lurking about in your skull, because I don't have a clue. I've never met another person quite like you."

"Ditto, Andi," he said, "to everything you just said."

"I suppose that means we'll have to—"

Two loud cracks, followed by a series of short, echoing blasts hit Andi's ears with sudden force. She forgot, instantly, where she was. Her chest tightened until she could hardly breathe, her vision blurred and her pulse took on the speed of the winning horse at the Kentucky

Derby. The ground beneath her feet thinned, became wobbly, and beads of fear-induced sweat gathered at her hairline. She was less than thirty seconds from a complete meltdown, otherwise known as a panic attack.

Okay. Okay. She knew how to handle these, had even found success a few times. The noise…it wasn't gunfire. She was not in Juliana Memorial Hospital, and she had not been shot. Hugh wasn't lying on the floor in front of her, dead or dying. She wasn't there, she was here. She was safe. *Safe*, damn it! Rational, true words. Unfortunately, despite their accuracy, they did not connect with her emotion. They did not alter the terror running through her blood.

Thoughts in a jumble, she brought to mind the next step that she'd learned while in counseling. Connect with the real world, breathe deeply, find a center…a balance.

Forcing her eyes wide open, she focused on Ryan. His concern was obvious as he watched her carefully and appeared primed and ready to catch her or hold her or…something, if she were to fall or freak out or collapse. "Panic attack," she mumbled. "I'm trying to get it under control before it takes over. But—"

She gasped when another series of loud blasts went off, ricocheting through the air and tying the rest of her stomach into hard, impenetrable knots.

"Listen to my voice. Look at *me*." Ryan's hands were on her shoulders, guiding her body closer to his. "Fireworks. That's what you're hearing, what your body is mistaking for danger. But there isn't anything to be afraid of. I promise. Just breathe. Look at me and breathe."

"Fireworks," she said, doing as Ryan requested. Her

eyes found his, and she felt safer. Her courage strength-ened. The real world came into true-blue focus and Juli-ana Memorial Hospital, along with the image of Hugh, faded. "Just fireworks. Where are they?"

Carefully, as if she were precious and oh-so-breakable, he turned her around so she faced the opposite direction. "Right up there, Andi. I'd say that's a beautiful sight, wouldn't you?"

Bright colors saturated the twilight sky in long, streaky lines that flared outward until they seemingly dropped to the earth, faded and paled in hue before dis-appearing from view. "Yes," she said softly, the ground becoming firm, her legs steady again. "Beautiful."

Leaning backward against Ryan's chest, she didn't object when he held her tight or rested his jaw on the top of her head. She just breathed. In and out, in and out, and waited for the pounding beat of her heart to return to normal and for the frayed edges of her nerves to calm.

They stayed that way for a while, locked together, staring at the multicolored sky as firework after fire-work erupted. And, yes, she felt safe. Cared for by Ryan and important to him, as well. These emotions—as positive as they were—mingled with her attraction to-ward him, the chemistry that existed *between them*, and caused some concern, some doubt. About that at-traction, the chemistry and if the security she experi-enced with Ryan—his obvious care, her apparent value to him—had ignited her desire into being.

Based on her history with patients she'd cared for, the possibility remained strong. But, Lord, this desire she had for the man who held her now? It resonated so deeply, so fully, she no longer found any relief in the very same possibility that she had a few short weeks ago. Simply speaking, she did not want to believe that any of what she felt for Ryan was false. Unfortunately, ignoring the likeliest truth would only lead to pain and disillusionment and, naturally, a hell of a lot of disappointment. She didn't relish the idea of adding another layer of muck to pull herself through, and she hated that her uncertainty might even hurt Ryan.

He was a good guy. He had a good heart. He'd proved both in spades within the small amount of time they'd known each other. And while he did not require *her* protection—he was a grown man, after all—she refused to ignore how her current inabilities and confusion could affect him or his heart. Doing so wouldn't only be selfish, it would be cruel.

In this second, though, she swallowed her concerns and enjoyed every ounce of goodness that filled *her* heart and soul. Earlier, she had arrived at the wrong conclusion. Changes were, indeed, happening here in Steamboat Springs that hadn't occurred at home. An awakening of sorts. An awareness of herself, her body and the world—hell, the *people*—around her that had been missing since December. And tonight, with Ryan's help, she'd avoided a panic attack.

Yes, changes were happening. Positive, life-affirming changes. She couldn't—wouldn't—deny or ignore or minimize that truth, either. So, she'd…continue on, keep the good and the potential bad in mind, and wait until the dust cleared enough to see the full truth.

Whatever that might be.

Chapter Six

"So, Mom," Ryan said the following afternoon at his parents' house, "Nicole has one more birthday present in mind for you, but she'll need some time to get everything in order. Maybe a year or more. Probably why she hasn't said anything yet. Right, Nic?"

His sister narrowed her blue eyes and gave him a what-in-the-hell-are-you-talking-about-now type of look. "Um. I don't know what your addle-brained son is going on about, Mom, but don't believe a word he says. Now, I do have some ideas for Christmas, but that's a ways off."

"Wow! You think…" Purposely letting his words trail off, Ryan counted aloud on his fingers, and then said, "Six months? I know triplets are often born early, but come on, let's shoot for the full nine months. Eight, at least. To insure their lungs are—"

She smacked him hard on his arm. "You're a brat. Have always been a brat, will always be a brat." Standing up from the kitchen table, she started clearing the dishes. "Don't listen to a word he says, either of you," she said to their parents. "I'm not pregnant. He's referring to our ongoing jokes about how you'd like to be a grandma, Mom, and…well, just ignore him."

Joining his sister in picking up from their cake-and-ice-cream celebration, he said, "Excuse me if I believed you about calling one-eight-hundred-baby. You should really be more clear when you're joking, Nicole. I can't read your mind, now can I?"

Splashing water from the running faucet in his direction, she grinned. "You're such a pain in the butt. Unless something miraculous occurs, you're much more likely to produce offspring in the near future. Now, apologize to our mother for getting her hopes up."

And there it was again, the twinge of pain evident in his sister's eyes and her expression. He'd seen it yesterday when they were having a very similar conversation about…babies. Comprehension dawned. The chemotherapy treatments Nicole endured had probably ramped up her biological clock. Aw, hell. Now he just felt bad for the teasing.

"Hey, Mom," he said, facing the table where both his parents still sat, "I am sorry. I was just trying to get Nicole to laugh. You, too, so I hope you didn't take me seriously."

Brenda shrugged. "I did not take you seriously. Your voice gives you away when you're teasing or leading into a joke. However," she said, turning her attention to Nicole, "I am curious about your statement. Why might your brother produce offspring in the near future?"

Her cheeks a bright apple-red, Nicole finished rinsing the plates before answering. "Oh, I don't know. He's—for a pain in the butt—an okay-looking guy. I'm guessing it won't be much longer before he dives into the dating pool again. Women seem to like him and…

and…it's been a while since Leah, so it's just an assumption, really. Nothing concrete."

"Uh-huh. Jerry," their mother said to their father, "am I mistaken, or is our daughter hiding something about our son from us? Such as, he's already started dating someone?"

"Well now, it's certainly a possibility." Jerry stretched his arms behind him and clasped the back of his head with his hands, taking on a pseudorelaxed pose. "Our daughter has never excelled at duplicity, as you know. That being said, Ryan is usually quick to tell us if something has changed in his life. I don't know, Brenda. Could go either way here."

"Sorry, Ryan," Nicole said half under her breath. "Didn't mean to put you in hot water."

"It's okay," he said, not bothering to lower his voice. "I'm not in hot water, but I do have a private life. And, yup, while I've often confided in the beginning stages of anything new, relationships or otherwise, this is not a topic I'm willing to discuss."

"But there is someone," his mother said, her excitement and curiosity apparent. "That's good. And, of course, you don't have to share anything you don't want to right now. But at some point, when you're ready, I would like to hear all about this woman, whoever she is, and eventually meet her."

"If and when the timing becomes appropriate, then yes." Ryan didn't dare speculate if that day would ever come into being. Oh, yesterday had been promising… in more ways than one, but he knew that Andi was a woman who needed time. As far as he was concerned, she could have however much of that she needed, which was why he hadn't pushed her into accepting his invitation to celebrate his mother's birthday. He'd keep giving her openings. What she did with those openings was up to her. "Until then, though, let's leave this topic alone. Please."

"Serious then, is it?" Jerry asked, his brow lifting in interest and contemplation. "Serious on your side, at any rate, if she's not quite there yet."

Ryan opened his jaw to answer, thought better of spreading even more bread crumbs for his parents to gather, and closed it. *This* was not leaving the topic alone, and until he actually understood what existed with Andi, there wasn't a reason to bring his folks into the loop.

"I know the feeling, son," his father continued, as if Ryan had verbally agreed with his declaration. "Your mother gave me quite the runaround when we first met. Lord, she tried my patience. Never met a woman so damn set on *not* falling in love. In those days, every other woman I dated wanted to settle down and start a family. None of them were quite right, until I laid eyes on the prettiest little blonde I'd ever seen." Swiveling in his chair, he looked at his wife. "So independent. Do you remember what you said when I first asked you on a date?"

It was Ryan's mother's turn to blush. "Oh, I remember. I also recall your refusal to take no for an answer. Flowers and chocolates. Stopping by the house uninvited, helping my dad with the yard work and with his always-broken-down car. Bringing the groceries into the house for Mom. You were constantly there. Driving me crazy."

"Sure," their father said, a twinkle in his dark eyes.

"I wasn't about to let you write me off or forget I existed. Had to prove that you could count on me, didn't I?"

"You were relentless," Brenda said with a soft, light laugh.

"I was, and I'd do the same again if given the chance."

"Oh, come on now," Nicole said, returning to the table and sitting down. "You can't leave us hanging. What did Mom say when you asked her out that first time?"

"You tell them," Jerry said to Brenda. "Just as you did then, if you can."

"You're a silly old man with a fanciful heart, but okay, if you insist." Sitting straight and tall, Brenda leveled their father with a you-gotta-be-kidding-me type of smirk—Ryan guessed you'd call it—and said in a voice fit for royalty, "A date? I'm sorry, I'm busy every night for the next year. You'll have to find someone else to entertain you."

"Mother! You couldn't have just said, *No, thank you*?" Nicole said. "Poor Daddy."

"Your 'poor' father was known for playing the field," Brenda said. "And breaking hearts. He was quite the ladies' man, whether he wants to admit to that fact or not."

"Only because I was desperate to find the partner I yearned for. And then I saw you, and my heart told me everything I needed to know." Leaning over, he kissed Brenda's cheek. "It just took a lot of work, a lot of patience and a lot of convincing for you to see that I was right."

Persistence. Stubbornness. Determination. Yup. That sounded like the man who'd raised him. "Strange, we've never heard this story before," Ryan said. "It's a good one. And I'm relieved that you didn't give up and that Mom came around. How long did it take?"

"Not too long, considering where we started." Jerry winked at Brenda. "Less than six months, wasn't it, before you started to thaw? Or am I remembering incorrectly?"

Brenda sniffed. "Only took three months, I just kept you waiting for another two to see how serious you actually were," she said, a sparkle in her baby blues. "By then, I knew without a doubt that I'd marry you someday and that we would make an excellent team."

Huh. Five months until his mother had admitted that his father had erased her doubts and allowed him to sweep her off her feet. Different scenario, by far, than what was happening with Andi. But still…five months. Didn't seem that long in the scheme of a lifetime together. Wasn't that long, period. Except, Andi's time in Steamboat Springs would come to an end when summer did. In roughly two months.

Sixty days, give or take, to help Andi stand one hundred percent on her own, in her strength, so she could vanquish her nightmares, her fears. So she could leave Steamboat Springs a freer woman who walked in sunlight instead of darkness. That, right there, was the only end goal that mattered. He wanted her happy. Alive. Hopeful.

And if in that space of sixty days, give or take, he determined that all he felt for this woman was true and real and solid? Well, that would be a gift. Even if he fell hopelessly in love and she left him here, without so much as a backward glance. But he'd be fine.

Of course he would.

As long as he knew that she had stepped from the

shadows and returned to the world of the living. That she had found whatever peace she required to regain her confidence. Yeah, that was a big one. And that she was happy. Really, that was all he needed to be okay.

Stretched out on a lounge chair the following Thursday, enjoying the late-morning air, Andi sipped her coffee and tried to summon the courage for what she planned to do that afternoon. Drive. In a car. By herself. Oh, she didn't expect to go far…just to the library to check out a few books, maybe stop at the pub and eat lunch. Say hi to whichever of her cousins might be there and feel…normal. No. Not *feel* normal.

Be normal.

And if she handled the excursion well, then later in the week she'd visit the magical hot spring again, with her camera and a book and whatever else she felt like bringing—and whatever she could carry while maneuvering the path—with her. But driving to Ryan's was a fair distance longer than to the library and Foster's Pub and Grill. So, she'd start with the manageable, see how that went and plan accordingly. Baby steps, yes, but in the right direction.

At the moment, the house was empty. Paul and Margaret had left for the pub about an hour ago, to do whatever was required to open for the day. Since Andi's arrival, one of them had left early while the other had waited until midafternoon. Andi's assumption was they hadn't wanted to leave her alone until they felt she'd settled into her new surroundings.

Sweet, really. Considerate, too. And for the first couple of weeks, entirely helpful. After a couple of more weeks, they were obviously ready to return to their normal routine and were comfortable with doing so. She was glad for both. Surprising, really, how quickly she had stopped feeling like a visitor and as if this beautiful house was actually her home. Due to her aunt and uncle's genuine and welcoming kind natures and their commitment to family, she had found the respite she so desperately needed. Still needed, if she were to be fully honest, in order to combat the nightmares that plagued her nighttime hours.

Doable, she believed. She was on the right path. Several nights ago, a few harmless beautiful fireworks had nearly sent her over the edge. But they hadn't. In one way or the other, she'd get everything else under control. One step, success, at a time had to be sufficient.

Oh, if she woke tomorrow a new—or rather, her old—self, she would consider that a miracle. Unlikely to happen. Miracles were called what they were for a reason. Therefore, she had to continue to stubbornly push toward her goals and be grateful for any amount of progress. Small or large. Today, that progress involved driving a car.

A positive step that would offer the added benefit of increased independence. No longer would she require her aunt to chauffeur her to and from Ryan's, and she'd have the freedom to visit the hot spring as often as she chose. Or to spend an afternoon at one of the many parks in the area, or take some initiative and stop by her cousins' homes to get to know them better.

Yes. She wanted to do all of that and more.

Andi finished her coffee and, ignoring the fatigue that penetrated deep into her bones, went to take a shower. Sixty minutes later, refreshed and prepared to tackle the day, she chose yet another sundress from her closet, slipped on a pair of sandals, tied her long mane of hair into a loose knot and applied a light layer of concealer under her eyes to camouflage the dark circles. Some eyeliner and a dab of lip gloss later, she was ready.

Aunt Margaret had left the car keys on the kitchen counter, along with a Post-it note she'd scrawled with the words, "Stop by the pub for lunch!" and had drawn a goofy smiley face. She didn't offer Andi luck or ask her to be careful, which somehow bolstered her confidence. It was driving a car. She knew the route to the library, and the pub was only a few blocks from there.

Of course she could manage such a simple task.

Dragging in a breath, Andi grabbed the keys and her purse and let herself out the back door. She was halfway to the car before she realized she'd left her cane inside, propped against her dresser, and she almost went to retrieve it. But, hey, she'd walked from her bedroom to the kitchen, from the kitchen to the back porch and down the steps without any problem. Until a few seconds ago, she hadn't even missed the cane. So…why use it?

Right. Still, she hesitated. Thought about the worst-case scenario, which boiled down to nothing more than tripping, perhaps falling. Embarrassing? Sure. But people with two strong and healthy legs tripped and fell on their butts all of the time.

Hell, she'd done so on more than one occasion when *she* had two strong and healthy legs.

Testing her weight on her right leg, she walked a few more feet. Stopped and grinned. Screw the cane. She only planned on this excursion lasting three to four hours, maximum. And a good hour or two of that would entail sitting in the car and at the restaurant. It would prove a valuable experiment, she decided, to see how well she did.

Maybe she'd learn she no longer required the cane, and that would be yet another positive step in the proper direction. Or she'd discover she wasn't quite there yet, but…even in that circumstance, she'd have the knowledge that she'd tried. And that felt positive.

Hopeful and affirming.

Andi slid into the driver's seat of the silvery-blue Prius her aunt drove and smiled even wider. Yeah, this felt good. She buckled the seat belt, put the key into the ignition and started the engine, inhaled a fortifying breath and, after the car was in Drive, lightly pushed on the gas pedal. Her heart did not race. Sweat did not appear on her neck or her hairline.

Okay. Good. But too soon to celebrate. If she managed the library and the pub and the return home without a whisper of a panic attack, she'd celebrate then. How? She didn't know. But seeing that the last time she'd attempted a solo drive, she'd had to pull off to the side of the road more than once in order to regain a modicum of calmness, her headway thus far gave her confidence that today she'd kick this particular demon's ass.

She'd then battle the next demon, and then the next, until no more remained.

The Facebook message from Leah might as well have been written in blinking neon lights. Ryan had, by now, read her words a total of four times, yet everything she'd said hadn't fully absorbed. She missed him. Their ongoing friendship was the strongest relationship in her life, which had led her to believe she'd made a mistake in ending their engagement. Could they arrange a time to talk? If he missed her, as well, and hadn't become involved with someone else, that is. And, of course, if enough care existed to possibly consider giving them another chance.

Well, hell.

Two years ago—maybe even as little as one year ago—his response would've been guarded but hopeful. *Yes. Plan a visit. Let's have a conversation, spend some time together, and if any possibility for a romantic relationship still exists, we'll take it from there. Slowly.*

He would've insisted on slowly. But, yeah, he would've wanted to see. To know.

Swearing softly, Ryan shut down his laptop and went to make dinner without responding. Oh, she'd know he'd read her message, would probably wonder, worry, about his delay. But he needed some time to consider how to best reply. Not *what* but *how.* So as not to hurt her feelings or cause her any reason to regret taking such a risk. In his opinion, risks were necessary.

Without them, anything that *could be* never *would be.*

In that message, Leah had put herself out there for him, exposed her heart and her desire to try to find their way back together. That could not have been easy for her; nor had she likely made that decision on the fly. So. Respect and honor and kindness were called for, because while he did not love Leah the way he once had, he still cared for her as a person. As his friend.

Therefore, he required some space to think about the words he wanted to say so she understood and believed his appreciation for the risk and his care toward her, but that, no, what had once existed between them could not be rekindled.

Nor would he want it to be.

In addition to his wish not to cause Leah pain, he felt that he absolutely needed to give her request the respect their past relationship deserved. He needed to mull through the reasons he did not believe they should, or could, regain what they'd once had, to determine the unadulterated truth and arrive at a worthy and compassionate response. All in all, it was a lot to think about, to come to terms with, to line up his gut knowledge against indisputable, honest logic. Especially as doing so meant revisiting the past, remembering the Leah he'd so adored.

A heaviness sat on his shoulders, clouded his heart, while he prepped and grilled a salmon fillet, which he paired with basmati rice and steamed vegetables. Over dinner and a glass of wine—he saved beer for pizza nights—with a sitcom on for background noise, Ryan thought about Leah. About the relationship they'd once had and how very much he'd loved her. How, at the time, he had set his various concerns on the back burner in order to convince himself that they were meant to be together. That no other woman could claim as much of his heart as she had.

Then, those feelings were true. Real. If Leah hadn't chosen a different path, he would still love her with the same strength, the same surety, the same confidence in their rightness as a couple. He knew this with absolute fact. When he loved, he did so fully, without pretense or subterfuge or doubt. Back then, no other woman— even Andrea, with her fire and beauty—would have had a shot at catching his eye or crawling into his heart. He just wasn't built that way.

But time hadn't only mended his wounds, he'd grown

and changed. With Leah, they would've—hopefully—grown at a similar pace. Become better friends, better lovers, better everything, as they walked the same path in tandem. That had not happened. Their paths had diverged and the man he was today did not recognize Leah as his other half. The partner he so yearned to share his life, his laughter, his burdens and his joys.

And while his instincts were strongly leaning that way with Andrea, she hadn't become that woman yet, either. But if she wrote him a message stating she wanted to take a risk and see where that could lead, what *their* path might be? His answer could only be yes.

That, right there, told him a hell of a lot.

But suppose Andrea was not in his life at the very moment Leah had her change of heart. What then? Hard to say with one-hundred-percent accuracy or clarity, because wiping Andi from his mind as if they'd never met proved impossible. She was there. Simple as that.

A different tack, then.

Say he'd received this message from Leah six months ago? His life here had been good, his business flourishing, his happiness at just waking up every damn day in this house, with the incredible view outside his windows, full and complete. He had not missed Leah. Had not thought about her in any way other than general curiosity or, of course, when they touched base on the phone or Facebook. Nope, he would not have had a different answer then, either.

Solid, confident and comfortable in his reasoning and his gut response, Ryan finished eating his dinner and moved on to considering what he would actually write to Leah. Simple was best, probably. The honest truth. He cared about her and their friendship. He was glad she had taken the risk to let him in on her thoughts. But he believed her original decision, while difficult at the time, remained correct. Their lives were different now. He was different, too.

But he wouldn't mention Andrea—really, what was there to even say on that front?—and on his end, he would try to check in with Leah here and there over the next week, to alleviate any embarrassment or oddness she might experience at being turned down.

Satisfied with all of his decisions, Ryan cleaned up the kitchen before returning to his laptop and powering it on. He had just finished typing and sending his message to Leah who, thankfully, was not online at that second, when a new friend request came through.

Clicking the appropriate tab, assuming he'd see someone in Denver—an old schoolmate, a prior coworker—or an acquaintance he knew here in Steamboat Springs, he was shocked through and through to recognize the thumbnail picture before reading the name.

Fiery red hair and a sexy-as-all-get-out, bordering-on-sultry smile. *Andi.*

She'd gone through the minor trouble of locating him on Facebook *and* had sent him a friend request? Well now, that seemed positive, didn't it? At first, all he could do was stare at the name, "Andrea Caputo," and the tiny picture to the side. And he had to work a little, to talk himself down from the probably meaningless request. Wanting to be friends on a social media site did not in any way indicate she actually considered him a friend or saw the potential, the possibilities between them, that he did.

But hell, if nothing else, it proved that he had been

in her thoughts to a certain degree. Waking from his daze, his surprise, Ryan clicked Confirm on the request and…just that fast, he had another connection to Andrea. It took some doing, but he resisted the nearly overwhelming urge to immediately go to her page and scan through her photos, her life before the shooting and after—if anything was even there—in the days, months, before they'd met.

At some juncture, he would. His curiosity about her and his want to *know* her wouldn't allow him to ignore pictures and updates that would offer a glimpse of her life in Rhode Island. Before he gave in, though, he wanted to see what *she* would do with this new "friendship."

The thought had barely formed when the "new message" flag appeared on his screen. Not from Leah, but from Andi. Yup, this woman was full of surprises tonight. All good.

Hi, Ryan! I hope the friendship request is okay. And I know I could have told you this tomorrow, but I couldn't wait. Today, I didn't use my cane at all, and I drove by myself. This might not seem like a big deal to you, but it was huge for me. I'm celebrating with an extra-large bowl of ice cream. Anyway, hope you're having a good night.

Ryan read her message and grinned. She'd had a good day and wanted him to know. Sure, everything she'd written was simple and direct, but he could almost hear her excitement, her pride in herself, for her accomplishments. They *were* a big deal. Both of them.

He quickly typed his response.

Hey, back! And of course the friendship request is okay. Better than okay. You know, I was actually going to talk to you tomorrow about your cane, that I thought you didn't need it for short distances. But look at you, figuring that out for yourself! And the driving on your own must feel wonderful. It's even more independence, which I know you're big on. Congrats on both, Andi! Enjoy the ice cream, and yeah, I'm having a great night.

He waited a minute, to see if she'd respond. She did, with a thank you for understanding and the congrats, and that she'd see him tomorrow, for their appointment. Another minute later, the little green circle that showed when someone was online blinked out. She was gone.

Probably to eat dinner or take a bath or talk to her aunt and uncle. Or whatever she did to fill the evening hours before attempting to sleep, only to be awakened by one of her nightmares. Then, from what she'd already told him, she'd spend the rest of the night awake. And alone.

Ryan hated that thought, the image itself, and wished there was a way he could offer her some company in those hours. He couldn't, without her reaching out, but maybe… Hmm. Without giving the idea any additional thought, he typed one last message to Andi. For her to see whenever she next logged into Facebook. Perhaps tonight, if a nightmare roused her once again.

A final thought before I'm off for the night. I don't know if you listen to music very often, but I have found music is a great way to connect. To feel company when we're alone. I'm just thinking that perhaps, after one of your nightmares (which I'm happy to hear about whenever you're ready to share), find a soothing song to listen to. Might help you relax. Might help you feel not so alone in those moments. Of course, I'd rather your nights were filled with sweet dreams. Night, Andi.

He hit Enter, clicked out of Facebook and powered down his laptop. Maybe, if she liked the music idea, thought it helpful at all, he'd share a few of his favorite songs, some of which had helped him after the breakup with Leah when, yeah, he'd felt pretty damn alone.

A glance at the clock told him what he already knew, that it was hours too early for bed. TV didn't interest him; nor did reading. Both were sedentary activities that wouldn't relieve his bout of sudden, unexplained nervous energy. What he needed, he decided after a minute of reflection, was some good, old-fashioned exercise. Yeah. He'd go for a run.

Maybe that would bring him down enough levels so that he could relax in front of the television or finish his book without a certain redhead clouding his thoughts.

Somehow, though, he doubted that would, or even could, happen.

Chapter Seven

Lying on her bed, Andi stared out the window, not seeing the sun, the trees, the pale blue sky or the billowing clouds. She'd had two fantastic days in less than a week. One in which she'd danced, laughed, beaten a panic attack and had almost been kissed. *Almost.* Yesterday, she'd regained a chunk of her lost independence by driving a car without fear or doubt and had gone the entire day without the use of her cane. So yeah. Two excellent days.

Today, so far, could not be described as excellent.

She'd had such hope when she'd gone to bed last night, such certainty that perhaps she'd sleep without a nightmare, that she'd manage enough rest to have a third excellent day. Instead, she'd woken within an hour, terrorized and sick and guilty, her entire body shaking, and burning behind her eyes was that damn buildup of tears that refused to fall.

But, even then, she'd tried to dispel the images the nightmare brought forth. She'd taken a hot bubble bath to soothe her nerves and eradicate her fears, had brewed a cup of chamomile tea and had purposely brought every good, positive, happy memory she could think of to mind.

Moments with her family. Their various vacations. How, as children, the Caputo sisters used to stay up late, hidden under one or the other's bedcovers with a flashlight and tell stories. Some funny. Some scary. They'd always fallen into a heap laughing.

Hours later, those memories led Andi to phoning home, having a conversation with her parents and her sister before they left for work, and she'd put on her bright, happy voice…pretending that everything was wonderful, that she was doing so much better. Talking to them solved the problem of missing her family but didn't do anything to help her mind stop circling.

None of her other attempts had proved successful, either. She hadn't been able to relax or to gain any additional minutes of shut-eye. Exhausted, drained, almost unable to function, she had canceled her session with Ryan, and other than brewing more tea and using the bathroom, she'd chosen to remain hidden in the sanctuary of her bedroom.

When Margaret knocked on her door, concerned, Andi lied and claimed a migraine, stating she needed rest. That part was the truth, anyhow, and since then, she'd mostly just hoped that somehow, her body would give up the fight and she'd pass out. Sleep for hours and hours and hours, and that when she woke, she'd feel better again.

Stronger. More hopeful and capable and not so damn fragile.

Yet, the bliss of unconsciousness continued to evade her grasp. Her brain seemed unwilling or unable or too vigilant to shut down, to become vulnerable to the images her subconscious was hell-bent on sending her way. Something had to change.

Now. Because she had nothing left. No reserves. No fuel. No…nothing.

Her options were limited, but she'd reached the end. If she didn't sleep enough hours between now—late afternoon—and morning, she'd phone her primary care physician in Rhode Island and follow her advice. And tonight, she'd give in and take two of her prescribed sleeping pills. Her doctor would ask if she had, and if Andi's answer was no, that would be her first recommendation. Smart and sensible. She should try them now, she knew.

She needed to, as far as that went. Yet, she wasn't quite ready. Even in her current state of exhaustion, she still wanted to sleep without medication. She'd wait until tonight.

Closing her eyes, Andi envisioned the hot spring, the way the steam had floated into the air, into the sunlight, and had morphed into magic. She thought of how the weight on her heart had lightened, how serenity had swept in and through her and had, for those precious, perfect minutes, buried her fear and anxiety and even her fatigue under a blanket of comfort.

Her thoughts moved on to Ryan. The soothing tone of his voice, the firmness of his body, the way he'd held her hand and how he had seemingly brought yet another level of peace to her heart. How she had never wanted to leave his side.

Easy enough to remember. To visualize and appreciate. But none of what she'd experienced that day reappeared in her present world. It did nothing to help her current dilemma. Maybe if she were there in person at the hot spring she'd feel some relief. But she knew enough not to attempt driving when in such a depleted condition, and her aunt and uncle were at the pub, working. Briefly she considered phoning Haley and asking her for a ride, but nixed the idea.

Other than Ryan, she hadn't admitted this particular struggle to anyone. Oh. *Ryan*. Could she, should she, reach out? He could still be working. He might have other plans, even if his workday had come to an end. But if he happened to be free, he'd probably agree. But, jeez, actually phoning and asking him to drive over here to pick her up, because she couldn't sleep?

Seemed too much to ask. This was her battle, not his.

It was then that the doorbell rang, sending her heart into overdrive at the sudden, unexpected noise. She considered ignoring it. Certainly, whoever was at the door wanted to talk to her aunt or uncle, not their visiting niece. But good manners dictated she couldn't, so she carefully sat up and pulled herself to a stand before grabbing her cane. Today, her leg was too weak to do without. Yesterday seemed like a million years ago.

The energy required to physically move from her bedroom to the front door sent shudders of weakness rippling through her muscles. Okay, maybe she'd surrender to the sleeping pills after dealing with whoever waited on the front porch. Stubbornness to get better without help was one thing. Ignoring her health, her well-being, bordered on insanity.

Andi unlocked the front door and tugged, struggled slightly—the door tended to swell when the temperature rose and, while unusual for Steamboat Springs, the past few days had grown uncomfortably warm—and finally yanked it open. The force of doing so, along with her weakened condition, caused her to tumble backward, nearly losing her balance. It was only pure good luck and the help of her cane that kept her standing.

"I'm sorry. The door sticks," she mumbled, focusing on her visitor. *Oh. Ryan. Here.* Probably to scold her for missing their scheduled appointment. Or to check on her. Or both. Didn't matter which, really. Here he was, as if her thoughts alone had summoned his presence, looking too good to be real. A mirage. One with strong arms, a sexy physique and, yes, those dark chocolate, all-seeing eyes she could drown in. Trouble. Danger. Security and comfort.

All wrapped up in a pair of formfitting blue jeans and a dark blue T-shirt.

She blinked to ascertain he wasn't a mirage. And no, he wasn't. Relief, swift and sure and far too strong for her liking, came into being. She scowled, pushed the relief down deep, and said, "Hi, Ryan. What brings you to my neck of the woods without any advance notice?"

"Hello to you, too," he said with that charming, semi-sarcastic grin. A cover, she guessed, for his concern. His nosiness. Whatever his motive for being here. "You're happy to see me, huh? That's good to know, because I'm happy to see you."

"Let me repeat," she said, trying hard to hang on to her defenses. "Why are you here?"

"I was worried," he said. "And from the looks of you, I had a right to be."

"I'm fine."

"Hmm. Yes, and 'fine' is Andi for 'I'm not fine, but I refuse to admit that or explain why, so please accept my answer and go away.'" He leaned his long, firm body against the inside of the door and crossed his arms in a relaxed posture. "I'm on to you, Andi. You're not fine."

"I had a migraine," she said, using the same lie she had with her aunt. "But I'm doing much better now. Really, nothing here for you to concern yourself over."

"You're here, aren't you? I'm concerned for you." His voice was quiet, calm. Steady. "And you look as if you're less than thirty seconds from keeling over and dropping to the floor in a heap."

"Migraine," she insisted. "I don't get them often, but—"

"Stop. Please," he said. "Do me the honor of telling the truth."

Damn it. "Haven't slept more than an hour. Not since the night before last, and that was my…three-hour norm. But I have a plan now, see, and really, there isn't any need to burden yourself or go out of your way. I…have it figured out. And—"

"Nothing to do with you is a burden." He pushed out a breath. "Invite me in or we can sit out here, on the porch. But we're going to talk, and you need to get off your feet."

"There isn't anything to talk about."

"Andi. Stop doing that," he said, his gaze and voice unflinching. "I'm not leaving."

She wondered, briefly, if she could summon the strength to push him far enough back to allow her to close the door. If so, she'd return to her bedroom and, rather than dredge deep enough to locate the will to have an actual conversation—*this* conversation—she could…what? Lie there on her bed and stare out the window some more? Feel alone? Feel…helpless?

Lord, no. She needed help. Had already admitted that to herself, and if Ryan could offer a solution other than unwanted medication or a call to her physician, well…that was by far Andi's preferred route. And yes, she trusted Ryan on an innate, hard-to-define level. He would listen. He would offer his opinion. He'd also said he wanted them to work on this together.

So. Okay. She'd talk. Really, how difficult could it be?

Decision made, she nodded. "Come inside, I guess." Giving him room to enter, she waited until he passed behind her to shove the swollen door shut. "We'll sit in the living room. Can I… Do you want anything to drink? Or eat? I can probably—"

"Nope," he said, interrupting her. "I want to talk. To you."

Nodding again, she led the way through the arched opening to the living room and headed straight for the comfortable leather-framed sofa. She dropped onto one of the oversize, burgundy-fabric-covered cushions, assuming Ryan would choose one of the chairs across from her, on the other side of the coffee table. She should've known better.

He did not. He sat next to her, smack in the middle of the sofa, and reached for her hand. Revel in his touch—in the warmth and the security of his body flowing into hers, by the simple act of skin meeting skin—or insist on her independence and yank free of his grasp? Warring instincts. Battling wants. Opposing desires. Where did the truth reside?

The answer, in this precise second, escaped Andi.

Ridiculous and perhaps a mite foolhardy, as well, but she went with the need in her heart. The demand to accept what Ryan so freely, so easily seemed to give. Swallowing a sigh, she soaked in the comfort that her hand being held by Ryan's brought, the peace that being near him ignited, and inch by inch, her tension eased and her body started to relax.

Miraculous, really, that this man had such a profound effect on her.

"Tell me," he said, his tenor even. Calm and steady and…annoyingly obstinate. "What's going on? Why haven't you managed more than an hour's sleep since the night before last? Let me in, Andi, because I'm not going anywhere until you do."

"If I tell you to leave, you'll leave," she said, her mule-headedness kicking in despite her decision to do just as he'd asked, to let him in. "I feel as if I've been trampled by a…a herd of drunken elephants. Repeatedly. I can't even think, Ryan, so you need to realize that, at this point, I'm fragile. I'll…yes, I'll attempt to talk to you about this, but don't push. Please."

"I can promise you that I'm not leaving," he said. "Because you *will* end up in the hospital if we don't get this under control. But you already know that, don't you? And I can see you're fragile, barely holding yourself together, and I'm sorry. I hate that you feel this way, that you're struggling. I'm glad you've decided to try. So where do we start?"

All at once, the practical reasons to confide in Ryan melted into nothingness. She yearned to open up, to truly let him in, to be known *by* him. Because it was this man, *Ryan*, who beckoned to her loneliness, her bruised soul, a great deal more than the hope for relief. Why him? She didn't know; didn't dare speculate. But maybe the whys were meaningless.

Maybe what mattered most was the recognition.

"I don't know where to start," she admitted. "Or what words to use."

"Just…talk. Whatever is in your head, say it."

"Huh. Easier said than done."

"I'm right here, Andi," he said. "Ready to listen. To help, if I can. All you have to do is try." She felt, more than saw, him pivot his body toward her. "Would it make any of this easier if I asked questions or prodded you along or… What will help the most? You tell me."

Questions? *No.* Prodding? No to that, as well. "I think it would be better for me to get everything out in one fell swoop. I'm afraid if you ask questions or… even offer much more than basic input while I'm feeling my way through, I'll get cold feet. Well, colder feet, I guess."

A small laugh reached her ears. "You say the cutest things, but I get it. Go ahead, whenever you're ready. I'll sit here and listen until you're done."

Right. Okay, then. Where to start? Maybe before the beginning, before everything turned to hell, to her—quite literally now—worst nightmare. If she began there, perhaps the remainder would flow naturally, without any roadblocks obstructing her words. Maybe. Maybe not.

But it gave her an easy, nonstressful time frame to focus on.

"Christmas was about a week away, and it was a Friday. That night, a friend was having a party, so I had a bunch of errands to do before going into work. It was a…nice morning," she said, remembering those last hours before the storm. "I stopped and had a coffee. Sang to Christmas carols in the car. Bought a few last-minute gifts and…well, I was dating someone then.

We talked, agreed what time he'd pick me up after my shift. I was happy."

Ryan's grip on her hand tightened slightly at the same moment she mentioned she'd been seeing someone, but he stuck to his word and didn't voice any questions. She considered talking about Greg, explain what had occurred between them, but realized that would be an easy out. For her. Greg's presence, and then his departure, from her life held little significance, if any at all. And therefore, focusing on him would just become another form of avoidance.

"I got to work almost thirty minutes early," she said, forcing herself to continue. "Sat in the break room and chatted with…" Hugh. He'd been enjoying a late lunch and had told her a silly joke about Rudolph the Red-Nosed Reindeer. She'd laughed. "Um. A few of my co-workers. It was normal, you know? Just a typical day at the hospital, like any other."

"That's usually the way," Ryan said. "One minute is perfectly normal and everything seems fine. Perhaps even good or wonderful. And then, the next is…anything but."

"That would make sense, wouldn't it? For almost anything."

"Almost, not everything. But this is about you, not anyone else," he said. "I'm still here. Still listening. Still on your side. None of that has altered in the slightest."

"I know. I do, Ryan, and I'm appreciative. Grateful. I'm just trying to…put this together. So I clocked in a little early, since I was already there and a lot of patients were waiting. We always seem crazy around the holidays for whatever reason. Busy. It was just… hectic. But normal."

She kept talking until she arrived at the exact second the first shot rang out, loud and clear and terrifying, sending a jolt of shock and fear through Andi's body. Then and now.

Oh, Lord. She didn't want to do this, did not want to purposely revisit or verbalize this memory. It came to her on its own accord often enough. Why do this? Would it really serve any good? Well. Maybe it wouldn't, but… it very well could.

Like it or not, there was only one surefire way to know.

"This is difficult," she admitted. Again he squeezed her hand, reminding her of his presence. As if she could forget. But, yes, the reminder served its purpose.

Swallowing again, she started to talk in broken syllables and halted sentences. She shared everything she had seen and experienced at Juliana Memorial Hospital on the December afternoon that her world had shifted angles and changed forever. She described the repeated sound of gunfire, the screams and sobs and pleas, the peculiar smell—that odd, hard-to-explain scent of the aftereffects of a fired gun, along with the stomach-churning mix of blood and fear and adrenaline and sweat—that drenched the air, making it impossible to think or breathe.

Or believe there would ever be an end to the madness. One minute, sixty freaking seconds, might as well have been a month or a year or…an eternity. And how, as those minutes piled on top of one another, her hope had thinned and flattened and disappeared into nothingness, even as she fought against such a tremendous loss, knowing that giving up in any sense was not, could not be, an option if she were to survive.

As the words poured from her gut, from her soul, her exhaustion and loneliness and sorrows and panic all bound together, begging for the release that crying would give. The great unburdening that shedding buckets of tears would offer. But the tears did not come. They just sat there, hostage behind her eyes, weighing in her chest and filling her lungs.

Why couldn't she cry? She needed to, damn it. Just as badly, just as acutely, as the human body requires oxygen and food and water. Yet, she couldn't. And she did not understand why. What piece or part of her had become so broken that her tears refused to fall?

"You okay?" Ryan asked. "Need a break or…?"

"No. If I stop for very long, I likely won't start again," she said softly. She'd already dived in, had already gone too far to retreat. Cowardice could rear its ugly head at any second. Better to forge on, before that happened. "I'm okay enough."

"All right, then." He let go of her hand and swung his arm around her shoulders, pulling her against him, until her head nestled in the curve of his neck. "Go on, whenever you're ready."

Right. The time had come. The confession—*her* confession—needed to be vocalized, listened to and judged. She didn't relish speaking one syllable of her shameful secret aloud, to anyone at all, but maybe especially to Ryan. This was her biggest regret, and the guilt ate at her, gnawing its way through blood and bone. What would he think of her?

On the other side of the spectrum, if any solitary person existed on this earth with whom she could release this particular demon, he was sitting next to her now.

In patience and support, holding her close and watching her with those dark, beautiful eyes.

Yes. She could go to this place with Ryan. Maybe she needed to do so with him.

"The rest of what I have to say…well, I haven't really gone into this with anyone. But, okay, here I go. Trying to be brave." Dipping her chin, she stared at her pajama-covered legs. "The attending physician that night, Hugh Keller, was a friend of mine. A good friend. A mentor, too, actually. He would tell these dumb jokes…that, you know, weren't really funny. But he put so much into them, you felt his joy and you laughed. I always laughed."

Almost impossible not to, really.

"I'm a better nurse due to him," she said, pushing the words from her throat, where they were gathered in a clump. "We worked really well together, and he… always had my back when the nurses were short staffed or we had a difficult patient or…anything from the basic to the out of the ordinary. He taught me so much in his kind, unassuming way."

Ryan brushed the hair from her cheek, saying, "He sounds like a wonderful man, Andi. He obviously impacted you a great deal, professionally and personally."

"Yes, he was a wonderful man." Emotion, strong and pervasive, rippled and swam in her bloodstream. She twisted in Ryan's embrace to stare at the ceiling. "He died that day. I…saw him get shot, saw the shock and fear in his eyes. Saw him go down. And I started toward him, to help, to do what I was trained for, but I was scared. For him. For me. For everyone."

"You know, don't you, that anyone in that situation would be afraid? Feel terror?"

"I do know."

A minute or two passed before Ryan said, "Is there more?"

"Yes. I saw him go down. Started toward him," she repeated. "I heard yelling, the command to stop, but I didn't. That's…that's when I was shot. It was weird, though, I didn't instantly feel the pain. When I did, it came in an excruciating roar and I realized I was on the floor. Didn't, don't even now, remember falling. And…and—"

Here, she paused to regain her equilibrium.

"What else, Andi?" Ryan asked, his voice low. "Tell me all of it. Get everything out."

Everything. Right. That is what this was about. To determine if doing so would offer relief, another step forward. Okay, then. "I almost lost consciousness, and there was a lot of blood," she whispered. "Enough blood that I knew, or guessed, that at least one of the bullets had hit an artery. And I went numb. Not for long, but I went numb. That scared me, too."

Shudders so faint they were barely noticeable shook Ryan's body. And when he spoke, his voice seemed to resonate with the pain and fear that lived inside Andi. "Of course you were scared. I'm terrified now, hearing about what you went through. You…could have died."

"I know that, too. I…looked over at Hugh. He was down the hall from me, on the other side of the nurses' station, you see, and…and—" she cleared her throat, inhaled and exhaled "—his chest wasn't moving and his eyes were closed. His pallor was white. I said his name, he didn't move. I said his name again and I stared at him, at his chest and his eyes, and nothing. I decided he was already gone, but I should've made sure. And I didn't. I...I..."

"You're beating yourself up, Andi. You were in a horrific position." He sighed. "If you want to know what I think, then—"

"Stop. Don't you get it?"

"Get what? What do you want me to see that I'm not?"

"I didn't push myself to make sure. Instead, I was a coward. I got myself to safety and called nine-one-one. And he...he deserved more, Ryan," she said. Whimpered, really. "So much more. From me. This wonderful man who told silly jokes with such enthusiasm, this man who was my friend and mentor, deserved *more from me*. And I failed him."

Oh, God, there it was, the awful, awful truth that lurked in the deepest recesses of her soul. Hugh, she was certain, would've done everything in his power before leaving her there, alone and vulnerable, if their positions had been reversed. And she hadn't. She hadn't.

Insignificant, in her opinion, that she'd been terrified, hurt and bleeding. That she'd had to fight with every cell in her body to remain conscious. None of those truths mattered. Nor did learning that Hugh had died within minutes offer any relief or self-forgiveness.

She hadn't known that then. Not for certain.

"I failed him," she said again, her voice broken. "And it's that moment I can't get rid of, that I dream about, over and over. That decision. I don't know how to let it go. How to forgive myself. If I even should...if I have the right to forgiveness."

She waited for Ryan to offer a laundry list of explanations why she *shouldn't* feel as guilty and haunted as she did. Why wouldn't he? It was what she would do if someone confessed the same scenario to her, and those words? They wouldn't be empty or said just to soothe. She would mean every syllable from the bottom of her heart.

So, yes, she assumed the caring, compassionate and thoughtful Ryan would utter the same. And, sure, she'd appreciate his words and the belief that existed behind them, but she doubted they'd soak in and change *her* thoughts. She had failed her friend. How could any amount of reasoning, regardless of how sound, wipe that slate clean?

"Aw, Andi, that's a huge burden to carry on your shoulders," Ryan said, stroking her hair. "I get it, though. I'd feel the same. And I'm pretty sure you already know all the logical reasons you should forgive yourself, but you'd have to believe them emotionally, too, wouldn't you? And that's tough. So, I'm not going to try to talk you out of your feelings."

Surprised by this man again, Andi said, "You're not?"

"Nope. What I would like to do is suggest a different perspective for you to view this experience from, and maybe over time, the logic will settle into your heart and take root." Pausing, he lightly turned her head toward him, saying, "That is, if you want my opinion?"

"I do."

"If you were somehow able to talk to Hugh about all of this, what would *he* say to you? I think," Ryan said, his gaze solidly on Andi's, "that's worth considering. You respected him, cared for him, and from what you've said, it sounds as if he did for you, as well."

"Oh." Closing her eyes against the barrage of emo-

tions, Andi let Ryan's question simmer. She'd given tremendous thought to what she believed Hugh would do,
if she had been him and he, her. But she hadn't considered his opinion on what had actually occurred.

"This is for you, by the way," Ryan said. "You don't
have to share. I don't need to know. All I want is for
you to find that alternate view. I'm assuming you knew
him well enough in order to have a better-than-average
guess, correct?"

"Yeah," she murmured. "We knew each other well."

"Good." Ryan released his hold on her and moved to
the other end of the couch, and he put one of the throw
pillows on his lap. "Now, while you're thinking about
this, you should stretch out. Relax, close your eyes and
bring Hugh to mind. Have that conversation with his
memory. Just…be honest in that conversation."

Drained, emotionally and physically, Andi nodded
without putting up a fuss. Besides which, without Ryan's
body holding hers up, she was ready to fall over. She
stretched out, put her head on the pillow in his lap and,
after Ryan covered her with the soft blanket that had
been draped over the back of the sofa, closed her eyes.
She breathed in and brought Hugh—the smiling, sweet,
fatherly figure he'd been—to the surface of her memory.

And trying not to feel too ludicrous or demented, she
envisioned him in the employee break room, where they
often talked, and started the conversation.

*"Hi, Hugh," she said, taking a seat across from him
at a small, round table. "It's so good to see you. And…
I…I've missed you a lot."*

"Is that so?" he asked with his trademark jolly grin.

"I've missed you, too. Always loved seeing you, talking with you. So, how have you been, Andi, my dear?"

"Not so good, actually. It's been rough, you know? Trying to figure everything out, get stronger, keep...the faith. And I've made progress, but can't seem to push past one specific barrier." She paused, breathed air deep into her lungs. "I...feel as if I failed you."

"Failed me? Now why in heaven's name would you think that?" Blue eyes narrowed in speculation, concentration, a look she knew well as she'd seen it often when he examined a patient, read over a file...tried to fix the employee coffee machine. "You'll have to explain."

One tear, then another dripped slowly down Andi's cheek. In real life or just in her mind, in her pretend conversation with Hugh? She didn't know. Didn't care, either. "I didn't get to you in time, and then...I didn't... I didn't do what I should have. I left you, Hugh. I left you lying there, in a pool of blood, and I didn't even check your pulse. I just...left you."

"Of course you left," he said, his voice crisp and matter-of-fact. "And that is exactly what you should've done, what I would've ordered you to do. You knew, in the way we do in this profession, when it's too late. It was too late for me. I was gone and, honey, you knew."

"Right, but I should've—"

"What? Risked your life for a dead man?" he asked bluntly. "No. You should not have."

"Hugh! Listen to me, and—"

He held up a hand. "You listen to me. You still had a chance, I didn't. The choice you made was exactly right, and if you stop crucifying yourself, you'll see the truth of this."

Oh, she knew that tone. And, yes, even though this

*was her imagination, she believed in these words…
that Hugh would really say them, if he could. "Okay.
I'll give that a go."*

*"Good," he said, his quirky, crooked smile back in
full force. "Hey, by the way, I heard a great joke the
other day. Wanna hear?"*

"You know I do."

With Hugh's cheerful voice resonating in her mind,
the greatest part of that one-thousand-pound weight
she'd hauled around for so long cracked, broke in half
and lightened. And while it didn't completely disappear, the relief was instantaneous.

So much so that she sighed in contentment, snuggled in deeper to the warmth of Ryan and the blanket
and finally released the lock that had held *her* hostage.
She allowed the bliss of sleep to crawl in and sweep
her away, to a place of healing, the place she so needed.

An hour later, Ryan continued to stroke Andi's hair,
her cheeks, and kept his body as still as possible. She
slept, seemingly peacefully. She needed to keep sleeping, and if that meant he sat here all night and into tomorrow, he would. His first appointment in the morning
wasn't until nine. He had zero doubt she'd wake before
then. So, yeah, his plan was to stay put.

When her aunt and uncle arrived home, he felt certain he could explain the necessity of allowing Andi
to remain undisturbed without giving away any of her
secrets. They loved her. They lived with her. They had
to have some idea of their niece's exhaustion even if
she hadn't uttered one word of her nightmares to them.
Knowing Andi, she hadn't.

Truth be told, his heart had damn near split in half as she opened up, spoke of her guilt—needless, in Ryan's opinion, but fully understandable—and regrets from that god-awful day. She'd coupled a terrifying experience with a high level of self-destructive emotion—a combination that would give anyone debilitating nightmares. Including him.

If he had the ability, he'd take on all she carried for himself. Naturally, he didn't. He couldn't. So he had gone with the best alternate tack he could in suggesting she consider all she knew about Hugh, and what he might think if she could talk to him. And he hoped she'd found success, had gotten the answer she so desperately needed. Based on her even, calm breathing as she slept, he would bet that she had. But he wouldn't know for sure until she woke.

And maybe not even then, if her stubborn, independent streak returned.

Stretching his legs under the coffee table, Ryan closed his eyes and allowed himself the pleasure that having Andi so near brought. He yearned to care for this woman in so many ways. Rub her shoulders after a long day. Bring her coffee in the morning. Elicit a smile or a laugh when something had her down. Pull her into his arms and kiss her, as often as possible, so she knew how much she was desired. Loved and cared for and… Wait a minute. *Loved?*

Nah. He wasn't there, couldn't be there, yet. But the possibility of loving Andi had strengthened tonight as he saw her courage and her fragility. Her soul. Yeah. He might not love her now, but he knew himself well enough to realize that was a temporary state of affairs.

It wouldn't be long until his heart leaped and took

that final plunge. A day. Two. Next week or, hell, thirty seconds from now or another five minutes. Soon, though.

And he hoped, oh, how he hoped, he was ready for the fall.

Chapter Eight

Yawning, Andi stretched her arms at her side and shifted. Yawned again and opened her eyes, wincing at the bright morning light and wondered what had caused her neck to ache so darn much, and… Now, wait a minute. She blinked. Why was she on the living room couch?

Oh. No.

Embarrassment flooded her cheeks…hell, her entire body, with tingly prickles of heat as the prior evening's events came into complete focus. Ryan had shown up, she'd told him…everything and then she'd curled up on his lap as if she were a puppy begging for attention. Then… oh, Lord…then, after her pretend conversation with Hugh, she hadn't behaved like any normal person would. Oh, no. She'd gone and fallen asleep. In. Ryan's. Lap.

Carefully, as if she were still sleeping, she rolled to her side to see if Ryan remained on the couch with her, and…no. At some point, he must have found a way to disengage himself, leaving her to continue to rest on her own. That was good. If he was still here, she didn't know how she'd face him. Not so quickly and not without a good amount of preparation.

But…wow. She *had* fallen asleep. She'd actually slept, solidly, without even a hint of the nightmare she'd had every single night for the past many months. Due to her confession, Ryan's presence or the "talk" she'd had with Hugh, which somehow felt as real and true as the sunlight streaming in the curtains? Or had all three, with her exhaustion tossed in, done the trick?

Would she be able to sleep tonight, without her head nestled in Ryan's lap?

Well, that remained to be seen. But, wow, in this moment, she felt *good*. Other than her embarrassment, of course, and even that seemed to be dwindling by the second. If Ryan hadn't wanted to be here with her, he wouldn't have been. Due to his compassionate nature, she had little doubt that he would've contacted her aunt and uncle, or Haley or any one of her other cousins, to make sure she wasn't alone…but he would not have stuck around.

So, in this case, embarrassment was a wasted emotion.

And, okay, she'd enjoyed his attention, his care. *Him.* She'd bared her soul and she knew with a certainty that defied reason that she wouldn't have done so with any other person. Sensible or not, a connection existed with this man, with Ryan, and had almost from the moment they met. Which meant she had some thinking to do. Today. And a few decisions to make.

First, a shower. A strong cup of coffee. Some breakfast.

Andi refolded the blanket and situated the throw pillows on the sofa, stretched again and, feeling more centered and freer than she had in too long, grabbed a change of clothes and went to the bathroom. She took a long, deliciously hot shower, her thoughts on the release that purging her soul had given, the imaginary conversation with Hugh and, yes…Ryan. Lord, that man was never far from her thoughts. It should be annoying, really.

But she liked thinking about Ryan. Oh, why hadn't she kissed him when she'd had the chance? She should have, wished she'd allowed her temptation to overtake her logical, sane brain. Closing her eyes under the hot streaming water, she brought her fingers to her lips and stroked them from corner to corner, wondering— fantasizing—that Ryan's mouth was on hers.

What that would feel like, the full sensory experience.

A hot wash of pure desire curled into a tight, hard ball in her lower stomach, weighty and full and…and tantalizing—so very tantalizing—before slowly branching out and up and through her body…cell by cell, limb by limb, until every part of her, from the top of her head to the tips of her toes, trembled from the need. This oh-so-tangible intense need she felt for Ryan.

Stronger than anything she'd experienced before. Ever.

That had to mean something, didn't it? Oh, she wanted to believe so, but how could she under the current circumstances? She was his client. His patient. How much of what she felt was due to the care he'd given her in that role? She wouldn't know, couldn't know, if she remained under his professional care, which meant… she had to sever that connection.

The sooner the better, so she could focus on discovering the truth.

Andi shut off the water and, after toweling herself

dry and getting dressed, clipped her hair away from her face and headed for the kitchen. Sustenance was called for, before she acted on her decision. Before she lost her courage to explain her reasoning to Ryan, so he understood that her decision wasn't to run from him, but to see if she could, perhaps, run *to* him.

Hmm. She probably shouldn't phrase her explanation in quite that way. She might scare him off, if she did, and make him think she was a crazy person with false expectations when, really, she had zero expectations. She just needed to define this attraction, this *desire*, she had for Ryan. Even then, assuming the best on both sides of the equation, she still wouldn't *expect* a single thing. But she might be willing to hope for possibilities she couldn't yet consider.

Yeah. That sounded right.

Stomach grumbling, Andi walked into the kitchen and stopped short at the sight of her aunt sitting at the table reading the paper. The house had felt empty when she woke.

"Morning," she said to Margaret. "I didn't know you were still here or I would've said hi before jumping into the shower. Going to the pub later today, I take it?"

Margaret glanced up from the newspaper and smiled. "Good morning to you, sweetheart. And no worries, I was tending to the garden until…oh, fifteen minutes ago, I'd say. And actually, I'm not working at all today. I thought we could spend some time together."

"I would love that," Andi said, pouring a mug of coffee. She grabbed a bagel from the pantry and a tub of cream cheese from the fridge. "What do you have in mind? I have a few…areas that need my attention this morning, but after that, I'm good."

"Daisy has some free hours this afternoon, and she wants to shop for new clothes for the twins. I thought you could join us, and then perhaps we'll stop for lunch." Her aunt waited until Andi had finished preparing her breakfast and had joined her at the table before continuing. "The other girls—Haley, Rachel and Chelsea—might join us, too. Depending on if they can clear their schedules. This was sort of a last-minute idea."

"Oh, I hope everyone can come! I'd really like to get to know the females in this family better, and other than Haley, I haven't seen any of the girls since the barbecue." If possible, she'd like to forge friendships with these women. "So, yes, I'm definitely in."

"That's excellent news. We should have fun." Margaret sipped her coffee and then tapped the side of her cup with her fingers. "Do you feel up to talking about what happened last night? Ryan didn't offer much of an explanation, other than stating you'd had a rough afternoon and since you were finally sleeping, he didn't want to jar you by standing or moving you."

Strangely, now that she'd had the discussion once, it didn't bother her to give Margaret a capsulized version of the truth. She told her quickly and succinctly about what had happened at the hospital with Hugh, her resulting nightmares and exhaustion, and how Ryan had been there to listen. How he'd offered his advice and support. And how she'd finally slept.

"It was rough," she said as she came to the end of the story, "but it's over now, and I feel like an entirely new person." Or rather, more like the person she once was, though not that exactly, either. But that made sense.

"Crazy how easy it is to take something like sleep for granted."

"Until you don't have the luxury, for whatever reason, yes." Settling against the back of her chair, Margaret released a sigh. "I've known something was wrong, obviously, but didn't want to pry. Maybe I should have, at least a little. Maybe then you would've felt comfortable coming to me or Paul. I'm so glad that you had Ryan to lean on, honey."

Warmth touched Andi's cheeks. Not only had she leaned on Ryan, she'd slept on him. And liked it. A lot. "Yeah," she said, paying a great deal of attention to her bagel. "Me, too."

"I'm here for you, Andi. I truly hope you know that."

"I do. And I appreciate it, very much so."

"You know," her aunt said, flipping to the next page in the newspaper, "Ryan was still here this morning when I came downstairs. He said you hadn't budged when he finally decided he should head home, get ready for the day. He seems to be a very caring individual."

And because her aunt was right, all Andi said was, "He is."

Silence loomed, but not an uncomfortable one. Andi continued to eat her bagel and drink her coffee, while her aunt focused on the paper. But...wow. Again. For whatever reason, her assumption had been that Ryan had left shortly after she fell asleep, not that he'd stayed the entire night. The thought of him sitting there, on the sofa, probably becoming more uncomfortable as the night wore on, seemed rather extraordinary.

Who did that, other than a mother or father with their ill child?

But Ryan had. And that reminded her yet again of

how he'd wanted to kiss her, and had even suggested a path of some sort to walk down with him. If she was ready.

Suddenly, it became of the utmost urgency to finalize her earlier decision with action. Why bother waiting? If she wanted to embark on this path with Ryan, see where it might lead, her choice was to start as soon as possible. Summer wouldn't last forever.

Andi rinsed her cup and plate, put both in the dishwasher and turned toward her aunt, saying, "Let me go take care of a few loose ends, and then I'm ready whenever you are. For shopping and lunch and girl talk. I'm…really excited. Thank you for thinking of me."

"You're one of the girls," Margaret said with a light laugh, "so naturally, I thought of you. And there isn't any rush. It'll be an hour or two before we leave. Take your time."

Already lost in her own head, Andi nodded and returned to her bedroom. There, she pulled up an old email from her Rhode Island physical therapist, with his recommendations for who to hire here in Steamboat Springs. Ryan's name topped the list, which was why he had been her first call. There were a handful of others, most of whom worked at a local medical center.

A solid enough choice. She called and asked a few questions, explained her needs and scheduled an appointment for the end of the week, with the promise that she'd have her medical file sent over as soon as possible. Disconnecting the call, she stared at her mobile. Ryan was next. She hoped he understood that being fired meant something good, something hopeful, and not that she was unhappy or disappointed with the work they'd done together.

Unfortunately, when she called, she received his voice mail. Likely, he was in the middle of a session at that precise second. She left him a hurriedly spoken message, asking if he could return her call at his earliest convenience, that she had something important to discuss. And then, mostly on a whim, she followed that message with one on Facebook. Just in case.

Oh. He'd left her a message the other night, on her solo-drive day, and…well. If she'd seen his advice earlier, she certainly would've given the suggestion a shot. And, yes, if tonight or tomorrow night or whenever her nightmare reappeared, she'd absolutely listen to a selection of soothing music. In fact, she was surprised she hadn't tried that before on her own.

But she couldn't deny the truth that stirred in her heart. She was glad she hadn't seen this message, because if she had and it had proved a success, she wouldn't have shared the smallest morsel of her guilt. She wouldn't have "talked" to Hugh. And she would've denied herself the wonder of a full night's sleep while being cradled in Ryan's arms with her head in his lap.

All of the above had propelled her to where she now stood: feeling so very alive, hopeful and…well, hungry—ravenous, really—for Ryan's kiss.

Rounding the last bend on the path to the hot spring, Ryan slowed his steps. Startling Andi, possibly panicking her, by an abrupt and noisy arrival was not the best idea. He also had the desire to just look at her for a minute, before learning the reason for the messages she'd left on his voice mail and Facebook. Messages he hadn't seen or heard until an hour earlier.

Due to a crazy workday that had begun at his place

with four of his private-practice clients and then continued at the hospital for one of his weekly stints, he hadn't even stopped for lunch. And while he'd dozed some last night, on the Fosters' sofa, tiredness had crept in as the day marched forward. He'd thought he'd grab a quick nap after work, but Andi's messages had changed that intention.

She had something important to discuss. What that topic might be, Ryan couldn't guess, but there wasn't any way on the face of this earth he would put off a conversation Andi deemed important. He'd tried to phone her, but the call had rolled directly to voice mail, telling him that her mobile was either powered off or she was somewhere without service.

Concerned and curious, Ryan drove to her aunt and uncle's house instead of heading home, hoping to find her there. He hadn't, but Margaret had kindly informed him of Andi's whereabouts—the hot spring—and shared that she was in good spirits. Thanked him for helping her niece, and said they'd spent a lovely afternoon together, shopping and talking. Oh, and that Andi had apparently awakened that morning within ten minutes of his departure.

He'd like to think her body had missed his touch, and that was the cause of her waking so quickly, but the truth probably hovered closer to the simple fact that he'd moved and, though he'd been careful and slow, had jostled her enough to rouse her from sleep. The most probable scenario did not alter how much he loved the idea of Andi instinctively recognizing his absence.

Not in any way, shape or form.

Pausing at the edge of the path, a mere couple of feet before the clearing where the hot spring existed, he drew in a breath and just…looked. Appreciated. Perhaps even loved, just a little, the sight of fire and beauty and peace. The sight of Andi.

She'd brought a blanket with her, which she now sat on directly in front of the hot spring. So close he'd bet she could feel the puffs of steam on her skin. Touching her bare arms, caressing her cheeks and her lips. Her chin rested on angled knees, her arms wrapped around her legs for stability, and her long hair was loose and vibrant, capturing and reflecting the sunlight in the same magical, mystical way as the hot spring itself.

Beautiful was not an expressive enough word to describe Andi in this moment. Her clothes were simple enough: a long, flowing yellow skirt and a sleeveless white shirt that tied behind her neck, but even so, she was this intoxicating combination of pure innocence and seductive siren, crackling energy and cool tranquility. She called to every part of his heart, his head, his body.

She just called to him. Period.

Okay, he'd had his minute. Standing here any longer, without Andi's knowledge, would be an invasion of her privacy. Her sanctuary. Ryan retreated a few paces, just out of her vantage point, and started to whistle—loudly, but not too much so—as he moved forward again, retracing his steps and giving her notice, hopefully not too obtrusive, of his arrival. His presence.

This time, he didn't pause at the entrance to the clearing. He kept walking toward Andi, who was now facing his direction, a wide—and dare he believe?—welcoming smile on her face. She patted the space next to her on the blanket and tossed her hair over her shoulder.

"You found me," she said. "I thought you might. Wasn't sure, though."

He almost said that he'd always find her no matter where she might be at any given minute, but hell…in the wrong context, that could come off as stalker-ish. Certainly not his intent and absolutely not the view he wanted this woman to have of him.

Smiling, he sat down beside her and said, "Truthfully, I didn't have to guess. Your aunt let me in on where you were when I stopped by after work. Can't really take credit for finding you."

One eyebrow arched in surprise. "Oh. You tried to find me at the house?"

"I did. I tried calling, but when I couldn't get you there, I figured a face-to-face might be best. Since you indicated that what you wanted to talk about was important."

Long lashes fluttered in a blink. "It is, and I'm nervous about your response," she admitted, altering her gaze to the hot spring. "But…okay, you'll understand. I mean, I think you will, and maybe you'll even be happy I made this choice. For…um, the reasoning behind."

"I'll be happy, regardless, if your decision makes you happy." And he meant those words, but…hell. She was going home sooner than planned. That was the first thought that hit Ryan's brain. He didn't want her to leave. Not yet. Maybe not ever. "Tell me, Andi. What choice?"

"Well…the thing is, I'm firing you. Effective immediately," she said, still staring straight ahead. He couldn't see her eyes, her expression. And he wanted—needed—to see both. "I have an appointment on Friday, at Creek Wood Medical Center. I'll need copies of my file forwarded to them before then. Can…um, can you handle that for me?"

"Of course," he said instantly, his thoughts circling. She'd fired him—why, exactly?—but she wasn't leaving Steamboat Springs. Okay. "For where you are in your rehabilitation, Creek Wood is a great choice. You'll do fine there, Andi. I'll forward your file tomorrow."

"Thank you."

"You're welcome." Naturally, he was curious about her decision but kept that to himself. She'd tell him sooner or later of her own accord. Besides which, he had a few potentials in mind, one on each end of the negative to positive range.

On the lower end of that scale, he might have made her uncomfortable after last night's events and, therefore, she'd chosen to distance herself from him. A possibility he disliked—doubted, too, as far as that went—but couldn't outright ignore.

Even in such a scenario, though, he wouldn't change a second of what had occurred. Twenty-four hours ago, Andi had edged too close to collapse. A reality he'd recognized the instant her front door had opened. And today, she looked…still tired. It would take more than one night of rest to regain what she'd lost. But those dark circles weren't nearly as prevalent, and the translucent quality to her skin had mostly vanished. Her movements, as slight as they were, didn't shake her muscles. She appeared stronger. Healthier.

For those reasons right there, he wouldn't—even if he could—reverse time and alter *his* decisions. They were sound. They were what she'd required. And he'd give that to her again in an instant. So, no, he held zero regrets.

And on the higher end of that scale? All good. Nothing *but* good.

"Are you upset?" she asked. "Or curious, I guess, as to why I decided to end our professional relationship? Or… I don't know, what are you thinking?"

"Mostly, that I wish you'd look at me. So I can see you."

"Oh. Maybe in a minute. But not quite yet."

"Okay," he said easily, watching her closely. "Whenever you're ready. And, yes, naturally I'm curious, but, Andi, I am nowhere near upset. Why would I be? You've taken ownership over your body and formed a decision. I respect and honor that, whether you tell me the whys or not."

A soft, slippery sigh escaped. She gave her head a slight shake and sighed again. "I've known a lot of patient, good and caring people in my life. Male and female. But Ryan, I have never before known someone who exudes the amount of patience, kindness and care the way you do. These traits are as much a part of you as the color of your eyes and hair. Oh. Your optimism, too. And your sense of humor. It's like…I don't know, like you stand in sunlight. All the time."

"I'm honored beyond belief that you see me in such a way, but…I'm not perfect. I have my bad days, just like anyone else."

"Oh, I didn't say you were perfect," she said, her tone breezy. Sarcastic. And utterly cute. She picked up a small stone and played with it in her hand, rolling it between her fingers. "You're obstinate…frustratingly so, at times. And that smile of yours should be outlawed."

A laugh curled in the back of his throat. His smile, huh? "How so?"

"Let's start with the charm factor. It's way up there. Why, I wouldn't be surprised to learn that you've yanked yourself out of hot water on numerous occasions, solely due to…to how charming your smile is. In my opinion, that gives you an unfair advantage. Over everyone."

"Uh-huh. What else?" Lord, he was enjoying this conversation. Learning how this woman's brain worked, how she viewed him and his smile. "Gotta tell me the rest now."

"Actually, I don't. But…I will." Now she switched positions so her entire body faced his. And he was ever so grateful. Ever so happy to look into her eyes as she spoke. "When you smile, in addition to the charm, there's this layer of…joy, I guess, which makes sense if a person is happy enough to smile. But with you, it's bigger, bolder. Warmer and all encompassing."

"I fail to understand your logic. Why is a…joyful smile bad?"

"Not bad," she said quickly, "Just unfair and…no. Let me finish, before my courage evaporates." Pale pink shaded the delicate, lovely line of her cheeks. "The rest of what I have to say will lead directly into why I made the decision I did. We need to talk about that."

Awareness and instinct roared to life, burning in his gut like wildfire, ordering him to pay complete attention to Andi, to this moment. To whatever might happen next. It would be important. Significant. But he also had the strong sense that if he moved too fast, said the wrong words, she'd jump. Bolt like a rabbit. And this moment would disappear.

Perhaps forever.

Playing it light, he shrugged and gave her hair a gentle tug. "There's more?" he asked. "In addition to the get-out-of-jail-free charm and the big-and-bold joy?"

"Yes." The pink darkened, bloomed into a long-stemmed red rose. And his heart lurched, the heat in stomach expanded. "It's like this," she said. "You smile at me and...and my body responds."

Now that was interesting. Enlightening. Exciting. Not to mention enticing as all get-out. Still he kept with the light, teasing routine. Better for her peace of mind—so she'd keep talking, keep letting him in—and better for his, too, so he didn't take that leap just yet. "What type of response?" he asked. "Nausea? Headache? If so, those are symptoms of illness, darlin'. I mean, sort of unfair to blame my smile if you're getting the flu. Don't you think?"

"Oh, no, you don't get to name my responses. They're mine!" Another toss of her glorious hair and, with her eyes gleaming with a new type of fire, she sent the stone skimming along the water's surface. "And I'm not getting sick. I don't have the flu. This is your fault. And your smile's."

"Forgive me, please." Holding his hands up as if in surrender, he smiled with every ounce of charm and joy he could muster. Come on, how could he not? "You're absolutely correct. Go ahead then, explain these responses."

"If you'll hush for a minute, I will."

"I'm listening. But I'm pretty sure that at the end of this, we'll determine you're coming down with a cold if not the flu. Or allergies, maybe." He nodded. "I'm gonna say allergies."

The fire in her gaze burned brighter. Hotter. Lord, she was beautiful.

"Butterflies. They're annoying, Ryan, with all the fluttering and swishing and diving around they do in my stomach. My mouth goes dry. I suddenly have difficulty breathing. Or thinking. Or—and this has nothing to do with my leg—*walking*." She swallowed visibly, and a shiver rippled along her skin. "Yes, your smile should be outlawed. Because, damn it, you're irresistible enough without that particular superpower."

"That's quite the compliment." Seeing Andi this way—vivacious and speaking her mind—was akin to a blessing. And learning of his effect on her? Well, that was a gift to be treasured. "Irresistible, huh?"

"In the annoying sense, yeah," she said. "So I had to fire you."

"In order to focus on my irresistible nature, I'm guessing," he said, keeping his voice and his body language firmly in the laid-back camp. "That's okay, Andi. I would rather do the same with you. Focus on you. On everything about you because, darlin', you have the same hold on me."

"And there you go again, being irresistible." She shut her eyes and straightened her shoulders, scraped her bottom lip with her teeth. Searching for strength or courage or the right words, he wagered. Or all of the above. She must have found them, because she opened her eyes and looked at him dead on. "I think I might want to step on that path you mentioned at the festival."

Just that fast, his lungs refused to take in air and *his* thoughts became a muddle. While he wouldn't describe the sensation in his gut as butterflies—more like hopping crickets—he couldn't deny the similarities to her statement. And, yup, his mouth? Dry as a sheet of sandpaper. Surely, if he had to, he'd be able to walk just fine…but he was glad he didn't have to put that theory to the test.

Because this woman he couldn't get out of *his* head was willing to give him—*them*—a chance. What more could he ask for?

Not one damn thing. Not yet, anyhow.

"You're dangerous, Miss Caputo," he said lightly, "because now, I think I'm the one catching the flu. Or a cold. I seem to be suffering from the same symptoms you just listed. Can't be a coincidence, right?"

"Probably not a coincidence, but I don't know…"

He gave her a minute to continue. When she didn't, he asked, "You don't know what? Tell me what's on your mind, Andi."

"I don't know what to make of any of this," she admitted, lifting her shoulders into a small shrug. "Because on my end, I can't be sure where these…ah… feelings are coming from. If they're real. If they'd even be here without the care you've shown me as my physical therapist."

Pieces that should've clicked before came together. Maybe they hadn't due to being blinded by his attraction, or—the better scenario—the concern hadn't reared its ugly head because he knew, the way his father had known about his mother, that this woman was special.

Ryan *had* worried about the probability during the early portion of his relationship with Leah. He'd let the concern go over time, but it had existed. Even now, with the possibility on the table with Andi, he found he still wasn't worried. He believed in what he felt.

Evidently, however, the idea troubled Andrea. As a nurse, she would be well aware of how patients sometimes misinterpreted strong emotion toward their caregiver as falling in love. For her, that concern was one hundred percent valid and due his respect and understanding. She'd get both, plus a hell of a lot more. As much as she would accept, he'd give.

"Ah," he said, "so this is why I'm minus one client."

"Yep. This is why."

Again he waited for her to say more. Again she didn't. He had the sense that a little reassurance of his feelings would go a long way, but how much of his heart did he want to put on the line? How great a risk was he willing to take? The answer came to him swiftly, leaving no room for argument. *All* of his heart. As much risk as proved necessary.

Right now, the outcome—good or bad or somewhere in between—lurked in the distance. And whatever that outcome became, it was essential that he knew he'd given this chance with Andi every available resource. If he didn't put himself out there, prepared for the worst, he didn't have a chance in hell at receiving the best.

"You were honest with me. I will be honest with you," he said in a decisive manner. "I'm crazy about you, Andrea. I might already be halfway gone, as a matter of fact. If not more. But I understand your reservations, and we can take this at whatever pace is most comfortable."

"You don't have the same reservations?"

"Nope." He considered bringing Leah into the conversation, but decided now wasn't the time. Leah was his past. And the only woman Ryan saw in his present, his potential future, was sitting right here with him. Down the road, when they weren't in the fragile place of new beginnings, he'd share the entire story. "But that's okay," he said, returning his focus to Andi. "I'm not standing where you are, and even if I were…well, whatever you need is fine by me."

Relief simmered in Andi's expression. "I'm glad you understand. I can't make any promises here. You know that, right? I don't know where any of this will lead. If anywhere. I don't want to give you a false impression."

"You're not. We're completely on the same page." He reached over and tweaked her nose. "I don't know where this is leading, either, but I would rather move forward without any guarantees—we get none, anyway—than guess wrong."

"Of course, you're right." She exhaled a breath and graced him with a smile. Now that smile? Far more dangerous than his. "You needed to know where I stood. And now you do."

"Yup. Now I do."

Then, because his arms demanded he do so, he pushed himself closer to Andi and slowly brought her to him. "In case you're wondering," he said, brushing her hair away from her face, "I very much want to kiss you. I'm dying to taste you, sweetheart."

"Oh."

"'Oh'?"

"Yes. Oh. Because before? At the festival? I should've said yes." Her voice now held notes of longing, desire, rather than nervous shyness. And the sound of Andi's desire, knowing it was directed toward him, almost knocked him senseless. "I've thought about kissing you ever since. Wondered, too. Maybe imagined what it would feel like, be like. Once or twice."

"Oh, yeah?"

"Hmm. Yes."

"Interested in replacing imagination with reality?" He touched her bottom lip, which trembled gently, with his thumb. "Because if so, we can solve that dilemma right now."

"Yes," she whispered. "I am very interested."

Ryan breathed in the scent of Andi—that same warm, sunny combination of coconut and lime and flowers—and lifted her onto his lap. He liked her there, close. Watched as another shiver, stronger than the last, rippled and threaded its way down her body. Out of anticipation of their kiss, he thought, rather than anxiety or embarrassment or uncertainty.

A good state of affairs, indeed.

"I've waited for this," he said, cupping her face with his hands. "But you've been through a lot lately. You're sure, Andi? Ready for this step?"

"Yes," she said, confidence instilling her voice. "I'm ready. Exceedingly so."

Well, then. No reason to belabor the inevitable, now was there? Capturing her gaze with his, he held it for one beat...two beats...three. He lowered his mouth to hers, and a soft, sultry moan escaped from the back of her throat, kicking the desire he already had for this woman up another notch on the thermostat.

Lord, she was lovely. Delectable. Delicious and, for this second of time, all his.

Teasing his fingers into the flames—her hair—he kissed her fully, wholly, savoring her tiny, breathy sounds of pleasure, the warmth of her body pressed against his and how well they fit together. As if, from cells to blood to bone, they were specifically made for each other.

Meant to be together.

And Ryan knew—God help him, he *knew*—that no other woman, past or present or yet to come, could elicit the intense hunger, this overriding need, he had for Andi. He wanted her in his bed, beneath him, her fiery hair in disarray, her body open and willing and yearning for his touch. He wanted her to be his. He wanted to be hers. Not just for today or tomorrow or the span of a year, but for the rest of his life. The rest of *their* lives.

It was an absolute, bone-deep type of certainty that he did not question or doubt. It just…existed. Solid. Sure. Pure. And more real than anything Ryan had ever before known.

He dropped his hands to the small of her back, pushed her tight to him and prodded her mouth open with his tongue. He *had* to taste more of her, right now, as much as he possibly could, as much as she would allow given their current location. She moaned again, instantly, in a long, languid…*throaty* manner that set his blood—hell, his very soul—on fire.

The taste of her—sweet as honey with a kick of spice just like Andi herself—saturated his senses and drove his hunger, the passion he felt, higher, and then higher and hell, higher yet. He wanted her, all of her—her brain, body, heart and soul—every inch of who she was, inside and out, in every way a man can want a woman.

"Ryan," Andi whispered against his lips. "We…we need to stop."

"Why?" he asked. "I never want to stop."

"Me, either." A gurgle of a sigh-drenched laugh surfaced. "And that's exactly why we need to stop. Now. But I'm open to continuing this…let's go with *exploration*…at a later date."

"Yeah, you're right. Of course." Ryan imagined

standing in his shower with the cold water on full blast, and…nope. Not enough. Not *nearly* enough to expunge the heat pummeling through him with such power. He pulled himself together the best he could and kissed Andi once more. "But you're good, right?"

"Oh, I'm good." She gave him a smile that could only be described as saucy. "So good, in fact, that I think if I have a problem sleeping tonight, it will not be due to a nightmare."

Embarrassingly enough, it took a minute for the meaning of her statement to sink in, and when it did, the demanding ache in his groin increased tenfold.

"That was evil," he said to the woman who was, in one second, an angel, and in the next, a temptress. "Putting the image of you, on your bed wide awake, thinking of us, into my head. You have no mercy, Andi. How do you expect me to sleep now?"

"I don't." Shifting off his lap, she stood and blew him a kiss. Also saucy. Also tempting beyond measure. "I mean, why should I be the only one suffering from…flu symptoms?"

"I suppose," he said, standing, "you have made your point. Fair is fair, darlin'."

She didn't respond, just went about folding the blanket she'd brought, her movements quick and efficient. Effortless. As if she'd already forgotten the moment— the kiss that had nearly consumed them both—they'd just shared. He knew better, though. Because in her eyes, in the depths of her gaze, the heat of her desire, her need for him lingered.

And it was then that Ryan gave up the minuscule hold he had on his heart, cut the few remaining strings and took the leap. Felt the plunge. Yeah, this woman was meant for him, and he would cherish her, treasure every second of being with her that he was gifted.

Because, really, what else was he to do?

Chapter Nine

Had she ever been—even before last December—*this* foolishly, unabashedly happy? It was not a difficult question to answer: *No*, she had not. Oh, Andrea supposed she'd come close a few scattered times over the years, but in drips and drizzles...fits and spurts. Nothing like this rolling, continuous hum of excitement, pleasure and, yes, pure joy that now seemed the norm.

Her life hadn't suddenly become easy or problem free, but in a way, the not-so-great truths—her still weakened leg, the return of her nightmare on three occasions over the past couple of weeks and the guilt over Hugh that stubbornly refused to completely fade—punctuated the good. She'd smiled and laughed more, saw the sun instead of the clouds, appreciated the beauty of the Rocky Mountains and had been kissed almost daily.

By Ryan.

Kisses she now craved, dreamed of and—a time or two—instigated of her own accord. Everything with Ryan just seemed so easy and natural, as if they'd known each other for their entire lives. They hadn't, naturally, but the feeling remained. And as they spent more time together, she'd stopped being nervous and self-conscious about her attraction.

What was there to feel nervous about? They were both healthy adults.

Besides which, he seemed to appreciate her boldness. The truth was, this man seemed to appreciate almost every facet of who she was, how she was, in any given moment. Outside of her parents and siblings, she had never felt so comfortable just being herself with another person. It gave her an amazing sense of freedom to know that she didn't have to pretend she was happy if something had her down. Or camouflage her mood in any way.

And while she hadn't yet decided what had built the foundation of this connection with Ryan, she had mostly stopped worrying. One way or the other, in one form or another, the truth would become clear. Until that happened, she had decided to just relax and relish the now.

This afternoon, the *now* included a date with Ryan. He'd instructed her to wear something other than one of her sundresses, so she'd gone with a pair of black jeans and a layered pink tank. He'd refused to tell her why what she wore mattered other than he'd planned a surprise based on something she'd once shared.

And no amount of quizzing, teasing or begging during their drive had served to drag the secret from his lips. He could be, when he chose to be, rather obstinate. She'd tried to remember what she might have told him and when, but hadn't locked on to anything.

So she let him keep his secret, his surprise, and reveled that he'd even had the thought, the wish and the want to do something sweet and unexpected. For her.

Stealing a glance in his direction, she drew her bottom lip into her mouth. How could blue denim and a plain, boring white T-shirt—untucked, at that—look so darn sexy? Didn't seem fair. Or right. Though she shouldn't be surprised. She'd yet to see a version of Ryan that didn't jump-start her libido, which ignited a whole slew of her own wishes and wants.

Soon she might have to act on some of them.

"We're almost there, Andi," he said, tossing her that sexy-as-sin Prince Charming smile of his. "Another five minutes, give or take, and your curiosity will be satiated."

"Satiated, huh?" she teased. "Promises, promises."

"Oh, darlin'," he said in the same teasing tone, "I always keep my promises. Without fail. I was specifically speaking of your surprise, but—" he angled his gaze away from the road for a split second to meet hers "—if you have another idea in mind, I'm more than willing to listen. Potentially make you another promise."

Hmm. His tone, playful and fun, fit their bantering. But his eyes? They were a full shade darker than normal, closer to black than brown, and weren't teasing in the least. They were intense. Serious. His jaw had firmed, and his arms—those sun-kissed, muscular arms that she loved being wrapped up in—had tensed as his hold on the steering wheel tightened.

As if he were talking about an entirely different subject than she.

Not that sex between them wouldn't be intense. It would. Probably more so than she could even imagine, based on how their bodies responded whenever they kissed. Each time their lips met, her desire for this man grew by leaps and bounds. Huge leaps. Incredible bounds. And it was delightfully, powerfully obvious that Ryan's hunger for her was on the same level.

Deciding she had read too much into his quick glance and the tensing of his muscles, she scooted a few inches closer, put her hand on his leg, and said, "If I come up with any other ideas, I will definitely keep you in the loop. Right now, though, I just want to know—oh. Oh!"

A sign came into focus just as Ryan flipped on the right-hand-turn signal. Rocky Mountain Trail Guest Ranch. A ranch. He'd brought her to a ranch?

"Before you say anything, let me explain." Clearing his throat, Ryan turned into the long, windy driveway. "I wanted to rekindle the memory you told me about, when your father taught you to ride, and at the same time create a new one. A memory for us."

"Ryan, this is…well, okay, amazing. And thoughtful." So very thoughtful. Romantic, too. But… "Before I get too nervous, what are our plans?"

"They have dinner rides in the summer," Ryan said as he continued driving. "We'll each get a horse, ride for about two hours, stop for dinner and then ride back. The sun should be setting by then. We'll have quite the stunning view, sweetheart. It should be breathtaking."

Okay. Instinctively, Andi clenched and unclenched the muscles in her right leg. She was stronger—so much so—but a total of four hours on a horse? Was she that strong? "It's been a while…as in, years, since I've gone horseback riding, Ryan. And wow, I love that you thought of this, planned this, and…and it's such a romantic, fun idea. But I would be lying if I didn't admit that I'm nervous."

"I assumed you would be, but, honey, I'll be with you the entire time. And I think," Ryan said, parking the car, "despite your nerves, you'll love this. You're more than ready. Trust me?"

"Yes." The affirmation flew from her lips without thought. It was true, though. She did trust Ryan. And, oh, she very much wanted to enjoy this experience with him. Excitement eased in, replacing her anxiety. "You're right. This will be fun. And romantic. And…a memory not to be missed."

"That's my girl." The words were said in a carefree, nonchalant way. As if they, too, had come unbidden, without prior consideration. His girl. *His.* She might like being Ryan's girl for more than just the summer. *Might.* If the rest of her pesky questions could be answered. "Alrighty then," he said, turning off the ignition. "Ready to do this?"

"Yes," she repeated. And she was, as far as spending the rest of this day with Ryan, but to the other question…the one she'd asked herself, the answer remained *maybe.* "I can't wait."

Together they found their way to the correct stable and within twenty minutes were given horses—Andi's, a lovely dapple gray mare named Star due to the white markings on her forehead, and Ryan's, a sturdy yet gentle seal-brown-and-white paint horse, named, humorously enough, Chaos—and after being given a few instructions, they were set to go.

Well. First she had to actually get herself in Star's saddle.

"Want help, babe?" Ryan asked.

"Think I got it, but thanks." With her left foot in the stirrup, she lifted and swung her body up and over, and with zero issues, suddenly, she was seated. No pain. Not even a twinge of discomfort. Okay. Good. Smiling at Ryan, she said, "See? Easy peasy."

"Yup, just as I expected." He followed suit on Chaos and, once in the saddle, said, "Looks like we're getting started. You remember the basics, right?"

Rather than a verbal response, Andi lightly squeezed the mare's sides with both her legs and, recognizing the command, Star began to walk, falling in line with the other riders in front of Andi and Ryan. "Seems I remember the basics just fine," she said. "I'm already loving this!"

"And that," Ryan said, bringing Chaos to Star's side and matching his horse's gait with Andi's, "is exactly as I hoped you would feel. I love making you happy. Seeing you smile and hearing you laugh."

"You know, that goes both directions. I'd enjoy doing the same for you." There was so much to adore, even admire, about this man. And those words? Well, they hit Andi in all the right ways. "But you're so darn happy all the time, anyway. On your own accord, without any help whatsoever." Then, mostly under her breath, she said, "It's that standing-in-the-sunlight thing you have down."

"Explain?"

Ah. He'd heard her. "You're there for everyone. Calm and patient and supportive. Giving the best you can, whatever is needed, with that joy I talked about before. I haven't ever seen you upset or sad or so much as frustrated. And it's wonderful, Ryan, truly."

"But...?"

"But okay," she said, gently pressing her right leg against Star so the horse would turn left, in the same direction as the rest of the group, "this sunlight you walk around in? It's as if you don't need anyone or anything else in your life. As if your world is perfect, just as it is."

Quiet, except for the sounds of the horses and the other riders, dipped into the air between them. And when she looked over to Ryan, her heart picked up an extra beat or two or ten because, darn it all, with his dark hair ruffled from the wind, the natural ease with which he rode Chaos, the strength and firmness of his body and the striking scenery tossed in for good measure…well, he could've morphed into a cowboy. The silent, sexy…dangerous type.

Damn it. Why did this man have to embody the full, complete picture of everything she'd ever wanted? Where were his faults? Surely, he had some. *Everyone* did. No one could be this perfect. Not even Mister Walks-in-Sunshine Ryan Bradshaw.

"Listen," Ryan said, as if reading her thoughts. And, frankly, she still hadn't decided that he lacked such a power. "And believe if you want, discard if that's more comfortable. But you're only around me when we're actually physically together. Correct?"

"Um. Yes." Where in heaven's name was he going with this? "That's sort of obvious."

"Sure, but it needed to be said, in order to preface the rest." He gave her *that* look, the one that melted her from the inside out. "This sunlight you insist is a perpetual part of my personality? Perhaps what you're seeing," he said slowly, "is simply a reflection of…you. Of how I am *with* you, Andrea. Of the light you bring into my life. Ever think of that?"

Oh. Just…*oh.*

Speechless by his declaration, the authenticity layered into the words themselves and the swirl of emotions both had ignited, Andi shook her head. *No.* She hadn't considered such a possibility. Why would she? *How* would she? And how could this man view *her* as he did? Most of the time he'd known her, she'd been lost in a…a storm, she supposed. Only recently, and mainly due to Ryan, had the clouds cleared enough to let any amount of sun through.

Naturally, that brought her right back to square one. To the beginning. To how they'd met. To his initial role in her life, and what—if *anything*—that role had to do with their chemistry, with *her* growing attraction and… more than attraction. She might be, could very well be, falling in love. With Ryan. Or she only *thought* she was.

The gift of clarity had yet to make an appearance.

"I'd say you haven't thought of that," Ryan said, picking up their conversation where he'd left off. "So, how about you do that now, while we're riding? We can continue this conversation later. Maybe over dinner or, if not then, on the ride back."

"No need to." Ouch. She hadn't meant to sound so brisk. Cool. "What I mean to say is, of course I haven't considered that I'm the…um…brightness I see in and around you. One, that would make me rather self-centered, and two…it's you, Ryan. Who you are. How you are."

"Easier to think that, isn't it?"

Yes. Because otherwise she might believe that Ryan was falling in love. With her. And as wondrous and exciting and…miraculous as that would be and feel, until she better understood her heart, she couldn't offer him anything in return. As of now, her plans hadn't altered.

In five-and-a-half weeks, she would return to Rhode Island. To her family, friends and, hopefully, her job.

To everything she'd lost and everyone she'd left behind, including herself.

Of course, if she determined that what she felt, what she saw, with Ryan was as real as the blue sky hovering above, then she would change those plans. Because then, everything she needed would not exist in Rhode Island. He, Ryan, would be here. In Steamboat Springs.

But she might not solve that particular dilemma within the next thirty-odd days. Or ever. It would be wrong, so wrong, to guess. Deceiving and potentially hurtful, too. And she would not, under any circumstances, cause pain to the best man she'd ever known.

Would likely ever know. So, yes, absolute certainty was required.

"Nice one, Dad." Ryan watched the golf ball fly through the air and land on the green a few feet from the sixteenth hole. They were edging into the end of their monthly Saturday game and, as normal, the senior Bradshaw was winning. "Looks as if you'll be buying the beers," he said with a grin. "Just like normal."

That was another part of their routine. They always stopped for a few beers after their game, the winner picking up the tab. His father's rules. Jerry figured that way everyone walked away feeling good about something: either winning or free drinks.

"Kind of makes me wonder if you lose on purpose," Jerry said, grinning right back. "Because son, I can't remember the last time you had to fork over the beer money. And today, the spread is wider than our typical game. Having cash-flow problems?"

"Nope. Doing fine in the money department." Ryan selected his club, a six-iron, and dropped the ball on the tee. Before stepping into position, he said, "And I've never lost on purpose, though I will admit my game is a bit off this afternoon. Long week."

Between work, spending every available minute he could with Andi and fighting a recent bout of insomnia—a rather rare occurrence for Ryan, but hey, it happened to everyone—he wasn't at his best. Had even considered postponing today's game but hated disappointing his dad. Missing out on spending time with him wasn't high on his agenda, either.

Ryan took his swing and grimaced as the ball barely made it onto the green. He probably should've selected the five-iron, with the way he was playing today. Oh well.

"Yup. Your mind is definitely elsewhere," his dad said. "My question is where?"

"Told you. Just a busy week. Nothing to…" Ryan sighed and returned his club to the golf bag. There was something—or, okay, *someone*—taking up brain space. Might as well see what his dad had to say on the topic. "It's… Well, there's this woman. Her name is Andrea, and she… I think she might be the one. *My* one. I'm guessing in the same way you knew with Mom."

Jerry paused mid-stride to look at his son. "I see," he said. "What's the status of your relationship? Acquaintances, friends, dating or an actual couple?"

"Two out of the four. We're friends and we're dating," Ryan said, already doubting his wisdom in uttering so much as a syllable. "Andrea isn't local. She's visiting family here for the summer. We met shortly after she arrived."

"Got it. Where's home?"

"Rhode Island. She's planning on returning at the end of August, in about four weeks."

"And you want her to stay." A statement, not a question. "Have you told her that?"

"Nope," Ryan said. "She needs to make that choice. On her own. And I need to give her whatever time she might require. Like you did with Mom."

Lines crinkled around Jerry's eyes, not in frustration but contemplation. "Every situation is different, and with your mother, we lived in the same city. I didn't have to worry about her leaving and never coming back," he said. "But let me ask you this. How is Andrea to know you want her to stay if you don't tell her?"

"Sure, that's a point. But…" Ryan shook his head. "Such a declaration could potentially scare her enough that she'll…bolt. There are other issues at play here, and—"

"Is she as opposed to falling in love as your mother was?"

"Nah. That isn't the problem. I don't think it is, anyway." It was a damn good question, though. Another alternative to mull over, along with the rest of Andi's concerns. "I guess I can't say for sure. It's possible."

She'd also mentioned, briefly, a man she'd dated in Rhode Island at the time of the shooting. What had happened there? How long ago had that relationship ended? Why had it ended and who had formed that decision? Too many questions and not enough answers.

"Well, son, for what it's worth, my advice is fairly basic—don't keep anything off the table. Speak your mind and your heart, back both up with your actions, and hope for the damn best." Jerry patted Ryan's arm in a show of solidarity. "Love isn't easy, but when it's right…when you know deep in your gut that you've found the right woman, leaving words unsaid will haunt you. Every damn minute of every damn day."

Good advice. "I've tried to show her, but yeah, I could be…clearer, I suppose."

"Do that. Only way to be positive that she knows where you're at, what you're seeing," Jerry said matter-of-factly. "And if she doesn't see the same, you'll know right quick. Would be tough, I'll grant you that, but will cause you less grief in the long run."

Ryan nodded toward his dad's golf ball. "Let's finish up here. I'm ready for that beer."

Another slap on his arm, and Jerry went to take his swing. While Ryan didn't agree with his father's final statement—he'd feel a hell of a lot of grief, for a hell of a long time to come if Andi broke off their relationship because he spoke too soon—the clock was ticking.

And nope, he hadn't changed his mind about risk versus reward. He'd rather throw every last thing out there and lose than continuously wonder about the what-ifs. So, okay. Ryan knew what he had to do, now he just had to decide the how, the when and the where. The words he used and the picture he conveyed ranked up there in importance, as well.

Despite the number of hours he and Andi had spent together, her growing confidence in herself, her health, the heat that existed between them and her delightful boldness when she wanted a kiss, Ryan could not rid himself of the nagging concern that she was closer to running for cover than she was in sticking. Staying. Accepting his heart and giving him hers.

Ah, hell. This could prove to be a mistake, but he had

to try. Before it was too late. Before she left him anyway, to return to her life in Rhode Island. If that happened, his chance at securing the future he believed was within their grasp would disappear.

Possibly forever.

"Thank you so much for inviting me over," Andrea said to Dylan, Chelsea and the too-cute-for-words Henry. "Dinner was fantastic, but—and please don't take this the wrong way, Chelsea—dessert?" She winked at Henry before swallowing the last gulp of her root beer float. "Amazingly delicious. Probably the best part of the entire meal."

"See, Mommy? I told you she would love it better than apple pie." Henry noisily slurped his float from an oversize straw. "I knew I was right!"

Laughing, Chelsea gave her son an indulgent look. "Yes, kiddo, you were."

"So, you should listen to me all the time! Like with the—"

"We do listen to you all the time," Dylan interjected with a teasing grin. "Morning, noon and night." He tossed a balled-up napkin in Henry's direction. The boy caught it easily and, with a flick, returned the toss. A game they played often, Andi guessed. "Why, I think your voice is in my head more often than my own!"

"That's silly, Daddy."

"Might sound silly, but it's the truth!"

Feeling as if some unknown topic of conversation hovered below the surface—a conversation not meant for Andi's ears—she repeated her earlier sentiment by saying, "Seriously, thank you for everything. I've had a wonderful time tonight."

"So have we. And the night isn't over yet," Dylan said. "We've been meaning to have you over for a while, and here it is, almost August. Time flew." He shot a glance of pure love and happiness toward his wife. And that look? It was beautiful in its simplicity. Giving his head a quick shake, Dylan returned his focus to Andi. "Poor excuse, but we've been busy."

"Not poor at all," Andi said, trying to ignore the yearning that had somehow slipped into being, smack dab in the middle of her heart. "I should've stopped in earlier on my own accord, but I've been busier than expected. For whatever reason, when I accepted your mom's invite, I envisioned hours of sunbathing and napping. It…ah, hasn't turned out quite that way."

Standing, Chelsea started to scrape and stack dishes. Dylan immediately followed suit and began carrying glasses and serving dishes to the small, connected kitchen. To Andi's delight, Henry continued to slurp his root beer float, trying to get every drop. God, he was a great kid. Someday, if the powers that be blessed her with children, she'd hope for the grace and wisdom to raise her son or daughter with the same qualities that Henry possessed.

Sweet. Funny. Outspoken. And…secure. In himself and his place in his family.

It was, she decided, the perfect reminder of what she'd been raised with, of what she wanted for herself. Someday. With the right man by her side.

A man who stood in the sunlight, whether he chose to admit so or not.

Oh, she was close. So close to giving up the fight and just trusting all she felt for this man, everything her heart insisted to be true. But damn it. What if her heart was wrong? Had she made enough progress with her personal demons to make such a call? She did not know.

"Sit down, honey," Dylan was saying to Chelsea, who had just yawned. "Visit with Andi and relax. You did most of the cooking. Let me take care of cleanup."

"And you worked all day," Chelsea said softly. "This is a team. We'll both clear the table, and then we'll get done quicker. And, my dear, sweet husband—" she grinned conspiratorially at Andi "—don't bother with your mule-headed routine. Just give in now and accept that I'm right, rather than in two hours or tomorrow or—"

"Me? Stubborn?" Dylan dropped a kiss on Chelsea's lips. "You must be thinking of a different guy, because I'm about as laid-back as they get. Help me out here, Andi!"

"Hmm, I don't know if I can," Andi said, remembering a specific incident from her childhood visit so many years ago. "Let's see if this rings a bell—camping with our families. Reid's desire to prove he could catch a bigger fish than you and Cole. And a certain someone who refused to give up on proving Reid wrong...all day. Into the evening, missing lunch and dinner, until Uncle Paul decided enough was enough, and—"

"I remember that!" Dylan said. "But you have the wrong person. We're not talking about how stubborn Cole is, and I'm almost positive he is the certain someone you're referring to."

"Oh, no. You don't get to do that," Andi said, laughing. "It was, without a doubt, you. Because the very next day, you were right back at it, trying to catch a fish bigger than Reid's. Want to know how I remember this so clearly?"

"Sure," Dylan said, "though, you were fairly young. Your memories could be off."

"They're not," Andi said, bringing that day to the forefront. "Haley and Audrey had taken off somewhere with Reid and Cole and your dad, and I was…lonely, I guess. You—as in Dylan Foster—said I could sit with you while you fished. I went with you. It's a nice memory. Don't muddy it up by being…oh, obstinate!"

"Okay, okay. You're right," Dylan said, relenting. "I tried to teach you to fish, but you had no interest. We talked, though. You told me, that long ago, that you were going to be a nurse someday. I believed you…and look, you never changed your mind."

She had told him that. She remembered that conversation. "Well. My point is this. If you were that stubborn then, you're likely ten times more mule-headed now, as an adult."

Chelsea snickered. "Try twenty times."

"Or thirty!" Henry piped in. "Forty!"

"Okay, you two, enough from the peanut gallery." Dylan shook his head in a poor-me, imploring sort of way. "See what I have to put up with? In my own home, even?"

"I don't know," Andi said with a shrug. "Seems sort of wonderful to me. Not sure you should be complaining, with such a beautiful wife and handsome son."

"And a baby, too!" Henry said. "Well, not yet. Not for lots of months, and only *one* baby, not two babies. That would be a lot of noisy crying and I know that for fact!"

Oh. Oh! Andrea glanced from Dylan to Chelsea, both of whom were staring at Henry with stunned but amused expressions. Obviously, this was information not meant to be shared just yet. "I didn't hear anything," she said, pretending to zip her lips. "Nothing. At all."

Henry's eyes widened. "That was spose to be a secret. About the baby."

"It's okay, sweetie," Chelsea said, leaning down to kiss the top of his head. "We understand you're excited about becoming a big brother and that it's hard to not tell everyone."

"Yup," Dylan said. "Don't be upset. We're not. We planned on telling everyone soon, anyway. You will be such a terrific big brother, Henry. Without doubt, your little sister or brother is so lucky to have you."

"I know that, Daddy." Henry looked up to Dylan, his natural grin firmly in place. "But she's a girl, not a boy. I already know. And I'll love her lots and make sure she's safe and stuff, 'cause that's what big brothers do." Scowling now and with a quick shake of his head, he said, "I'm not playing with any dolls, though. Ever!"

"She…er, the baby might be a boy, kiddo," Chelsea said. "And yes, we're probably only having one baby, but we don't know that yet, either. It's better if we just wait and see."

Shaking his head more vehemently, Henry said, "I'm having a sister, and there isn't a second baby. And I've been thinking lots about what to name her, since I'll have to talk to her and stuff, and I decided her name should start with an *H*. Like my name does."

"Hmm. Not a bad idea," Dylan said. "Maybe Henrietta?"

"No," Henry said. "Too much like my name."

"Hermione?"

Henry scrunched his face in thought. "Um. No to that, too."

"Hazel?"

When Henry didn't immediately answer, Chelsea said, "Let's round off the noes with a third, but I like the *H* idea. Keep thinking. Boy and girl names, though." She disappeared into the kitchen with an armful of dishes, returning a few minutes later. "No other thoughts?"

"I've always liked the name Hannah," Andrea said, joining the fray. "But to be completely honest, I'm a huge fan of old-fashioned names. I think Hazel is lovely."

"Yeah! Hazel, Mommy," Henry said. "Hazel Foster. That's her name!"

Sighing, Chelsea said, "What am I going to do with you, huh? Can we please hold off on finalizing a name until January, at least? Since she…the baby, that is… isn't due until March?"

"I want to know what to call her now," Henry said, tilting his jaw.

"Henry, sweetie, maybe when we know for sure—" Breaking off, Chelsea shrugged. "It's just too soon."

Wanting to help distract Henry, Andrea said, "Oh, no! I just realized I haven't seen your bedroom, Henry, and I can't leave until I do. Feel like giving me a tour? But don't tell me what color your walls are painted. I'm going to guess…blue!"

"Nope! But I'll show you!" All but leaping from his chair, and the baby-name discussion apparently shoved to the back burner for now, Henry grabbed Andi's hand and tugged. "Daddy let me choose what color I liked best, and blue is okay. But it isn't my favorite. Come on! You can see my race-car track, too. And my cars!"

Chelsea mouthed the words *thank you* to Andi. Smiling in response—she figured Dylan and Chelsea likely needed a few minutes to themselves—she let Henry tug her from the kitchen, through the hallway and into an orange-and-charcoal-gray-painted room.

"See! Not blue." Henry spread his arms wide, as if showcasing the entire area. "I wanted orange, and Daddy said gray goes good with orange, so he painted two walls orange and two gray. And he was right. I like it!"

"Definitely better than blue," Andi said, taking stock of the space. The remainder of the room was definitely furnished with a little boy's likes in mind. Shelves filled with cars and books and action figures lined the walls, a large toy box sat in one of the corners, and right in the center of the room, a racetrack with two cars at the ready. "Let's play," she said to Henry, plopping down on the floor. "Can I have the green car? Please?"

He bent his head to the side, as if considering her request, and then nodded. "You can have the green car for the first race, then we'll trade. It wins the most. And it isn't fair if you always win just 'cause of the car. Daddy says it's good to learn how to lose, too."

Yes. Someday, she wanted a Henry all of her own. "Deal."

She could almost see this boy that didn't yet, and probably never would, exist. Dark hair, ruffled from the wind, and gorgeous chocolate-brown eyes that warmed in humor and happiness.

Oh. And he would walk in the sunlight. Just like his daddy.

Chapter Ten

Well, hell.

Could he screw up anything else in the remaining fifteen minutes before Andi arrived? Based on how the past two hours had progressed, then yup, he most certainly could.

And probably would.

It figured that a meal Ryan had prepared—at a minimum—a dozen times over the past two years to near perfection would fall apart on what might prove to be one of the most important nights of his life. Thus far, anyhow.

But okay. He couldn't alter what was, so what could he do to salvage this mess of epic proportions? Other than tossing the entirety of the ruined meal into the garbage and ordering in, he didn't have a clue. And settling for takeout pizza or Chinese? No. Not an option.

He needed a backup plan. Why didn't he have a damn backup plan?

Because of his absolute, self-centered certainty that his menu of chile rellenos, Mexican rice and baked corn pudding would proceed without a hitch. That was why.

If he'd only allowed for the possibility of error, he'd have considered a secondary menu. A couple of steaks for the grill, a loaf of crusty garlic bread and a fresh salad… hell, he could put that meal together in his sleep. What had he been thinking? The answer, he supposed, was that he hadn't been.

Worse, the signs of disaster were there from the get-go. First, he'd set the produce bag the poblano peppers were in too close to the stove top, and yup, the damn bag had smoldered and melted, filling the air with the not-so-pleasant scent of burned plastic. Then, he'd over-charred the peppers, but rather than undertaking the intelligent action of admitting defeat, he'd decided to roll with the mishap and tell Andi they were blackened chile rellenos.

Because sure, everyone wanted a little Cajun tossed in with their Mexican fiesta.

While the peppers were sweating off their skins, he'd started on the corn pudding. This? About the easiest, no-fuss, no-muss portion of the entire meal, yet he'd managed to overprocess the corn kernels to…mush. Mushier than mush. What he'd ended up with was more like corn gravy but thinner. While finishing prepping the peppers, he forgot about the rice. Which he'd left on the stove, simmering away, which…yup, also became mush.

White, gooey and wholly unappetizing mush.

The final straw? In his zeal to get the chile rellenos in the oven, he'd suddenly turned into a klutz and slipped—on absolutely *nothing*—and the baking dish had flown from his grip and landed upside down on the floor. Yup. That had happened.

Basically, he was up the proverbial creek without a

paddle. And his boat? Shattered. Into a million pieces and, at this precise second, was floating away in a pile of useless debris.

Ryan combed his fingers through his hair, tension and frustration percolating in his gut. Why did he not have a backup plan? He *always* had a backup plan. Perhaps it wasn't too late. Praying for a friggin' miracle, he opened his fridge and scanned the contents. Did the same with the freezer and the cupboards and groaned. Loudly. Twice.

Unless Andi had a serious love for boxed mac-and-cheese, mediocre frozen pizza, cereal with flavored marshmallows or peanut butter and strawberry jam—well, his mother had made the jam, and it rocked—sandwiches, he had…zilch. And that just shouldn't be the case.

Everything about tonight ranked high on the important scale.

He meant to tell Andi the scope of his feelings, his hopes, and that if she wasn't quite in the same place yet, that was fine. That he would wait as long as necessary, that they could visit each other throughout the year, and perhaps by next summer they'd be ready to take another step. One that involved a shared future. All he needed from her was a willingness to try.

In addition, he planned on telling her about his relationship with Leah. And he wanted to know more about the guy she'd been dating last December. If she had ended their relationship or if he had, and in either case, why had that decision been made? What had gone wrong? Did she still have feelings for this man? If so, how strong were they?

Hell, yeah, tonight was critical.

A glance at the clock stated Ryan had ten minutes, maybe, to do whatever he was going to do. Confidence flagging but adrenaline pumping, he decided that his best course of action was to quickly clean the kitchen, spray a ton of air freshener and, when Andi arrived, take her food shopping. For steaks. Garlic bread. And salad makings. Pretend that had been his plan all along.

Lame? Without doubt, but really, he had very few choices at his disposal.

First things first. Clean the most obvious mess. Ryan dropped to his knees and gathered the splattered peppers into his hands, dumped them into the baking dish and tried to scrape up as much of the sauce using the same method. Hands coated and dripping, and mentally adding "change clothes" to his to-do list, he crawl-walked to the trash and emptied the contents. Stood. And heard a sharp intake of breath followed by…a barely muffled laugh.

Wincing, now remembering he'd told Andi to let herself in, he pivoted on his heel—almost slipped again—and for a blissful second, forgot about his two hours of failure, the god-awful mess surrounding him and his food-stained clothes. He forgot everything.

Because, Lord, this woman? Breathtaking. Heartbreakingly so.

Auburn hair, long and loose and sexy. Sultry. She wore the same sundress she had at her family's barbecue, the first week they'd met. That lovely, almost whispery in the way it floated around her legs, turquoise-and-white tie-dyed dress that brought out the fire in her hair and the creaminess of her complexion. The barest, perfect hint of cleavage, smoky bedroom eyes and soft, kissable lips completed the picture. Yes. Breathtaking.

In every possible way, this woman pulled at his senses.

And all Ryan could think of was slowly removing that dress, kissing every inch of her milky skin and making her his. In all ways. *His.* He hoped she saw him as hers. Or at least, saw that potential. Now, disastrous dinner or not, he had to find out. He had to take the risk and offer Andi his heart, show her the future he felt in his bones was meant to be theirs and be ready to accept whatever might come after. Everything he wanted or… life without Andi.

"Ah. Andi," he managed to say. "You're here."

"I am." She blinked, attempted to smother another laugh and failed. One arm, lightly freckled from the sun, held what appeared to be a cake container against her hip. She stepped forward, deposited the container on the counter, sniffed the air and said, "What… Hmm, what's happening here, Ryan? Looks as if you've had a battle with…your entire kitchen. And lost."

"That about sums it up," he said, putting the baking dish in the sink and washing his sauce-covered hands. He hated her seeing him like this. If he couldn't prepare her a meal, why would she trust her heart to him? Sucking back the sigh clogging his throat, he faced her again and put on a smile. "The goal here was to impress you with my culinary skills. As you can see, that isn't happening tonight. But this failure isn't the norm. I actually can cook."

Her gaze left Ryan's as she scanned the area. Her lips twitched and she gave her head a slight shake. Returning her attention to him, she said, "Won't take long to put everything to rights. Do you have an apron? Or if not, an oversize T-shirt I can borrow?"

"You're not cleaning up my mess," Ryan said. "I'll

get you some wine. You can sit on the porch, enjoy the scenery, while I...deal with this and change clothes. Then, we'll figure out the rest of the night. We can order in or run to the store and grab a few steaks to toss on the grill."

"Oh, no, you don't get to do that, buddy," she said, leveraging her hands on her hips. "This is the very first time since I've known you that I can actually offer assistance *to* you. And guess what? You do not get to take that away from me, from us. Don't even try."

Narrowing his eyes, Ryan took in her stance, the determined expression coating her features, and, while it shouldn't have been possible, he fell even more in love. Did she have the slightest inkling of her effect on him? Of how her refusal to walk away from something as simple as a ruined meal and a messy kitchen showed him *so much* of who she was?

No. He wouldn't take this away from either one of them.

"Okay, you win," he said. "I'll get you an apron. We'll work together to put this night back on course. Dinner. Some conversation. And—" he nodded toward the container she'd brought "—is that cake? I have an incredibly soft spot for...cake."

"It's my specialty. Dark chocolate stout cake with fudge layers and espresso buttercream icing," she said, grinning. "I hope you're a chocolate fan, because this cake? It's...decadent."

"Baby, I am most definitely a fan," he said, holding her gaze. Wishing he was holding *her*. "I'm talking about you, by the way. But the cake sounds fantastic, as well."

Long lashes lowered in a blink. That rosy glow warmed

her cheeks, and she dragged her bottom lip into her mouth. A little action, unknown on her part he was sure, that served to yank hard on his desire. She sighed softly, saying, "What am I going to do with you?"

"Whatever you want to do with me," he said, choosing to stick somewhere in between serious and light. "Nothing's changed there, Andi. Your call. Just like always."

Or you could love me, he thought, *and let me love you*.

Naturally, he didn't dare speak those words. Too much else needed to be said first. They'd get there, before this evening came to an end, and when they did, he wanted the moment to be right. Romantic and calm and…all about them and not his disastrous attempts at dinner preparation while standing in the middle of his chaotic and untidy kitchen.

On that front, he wouldn't compromise.

I love you, Ryan.

The declaration sat right there on the tip of her tongue, almost begging to be said. As well, the emotion existed in her heart, strong and evocative and *real*. Seemingly so, anyway. Yet, she wasn't fully there, couldn't quite get herself to commit voice to those three words…to all they meant and all they promised. Until she could without doubt, they'd live inside.

But, wow, walking into Ryan's house and finding him in such a state of…disarray, had broken at least one wall. Her walks-in-sunlight man was not without fault, which she'd obviously known. No one was perfect. But to see the proof of that, to be able to step in and help *him*—even with something as trivial as straightening his kitchen—had been a gift.

She'd surprised him. The evidence of that had shown in his expression, his voice, and that too served as a gift. She liked being there for him. Maybe, probably, just as much as he enjoyed being there for her. A partnership of sorts. Small but there. Real, too.

After they'd finished with the kitchen and Ryan had changed his clothes, they drove to the store to buy what he deemed they needed for dinner. Andi would've been fine with the macaroni and cheese or the frozen pizza, but no...he'd flat out refused. They'd cooked together, though, and that had proved a pleasure. Fun and relaxing and easy.

So easy. Again, as if they'd always known each other.

Over dinner, he'd asked questions about her relationship with Greg...why had the relationship ended and who had done the ending? She'd told Ryan the truth: she and Greg had dated for close to a year before the shooting, and he wasn't invested enough to stick when she was at her weakest. That was fine. She'd preferred knowing that early on, and as it turned out, she hadn't been invested enough to care all that much when he left. Then and today.

Now, since the evening had cooled quite a bit, Ryan had a fire burning brightly in the fireplace and they were on his sofa, side by side, eating dessert, drinking coffee and engaging in mostly meaningless small talk. She had the desire to lean in, kiss him and run her fingers through his hair, pull him as tight to her as humanly possible and...kiss him more, harder, longer.

But, strangely and wholly unlike the Ryan she knew, he seemed reserved. Contemplative. As if he carried the weight of the world on his shoulders and the most complex mathematical figures were dancing in his brain. He might want to have a specific conversation with her, or he could be worried about something or someone that didn't involve her or their relationship.

Or perhaps, he was just tired.

Regardless, unless he reached for her, she'd control her impulse to kiss him. Difficult? Oh, yeah. Maybe more so tonight than ever before. Partially due to those three little—no, huge—words echoing in her head. Partially due to the nervous, frustrated state she'd found him in earlier and her resounding need to be there for him, to bring *him* comfort. Happiness.

And, of course, it went without saying how freaking sexy a man he was. His strong jaw. His outlaw smile. His muscular arms and long, firm legs. His ability to see straight through her, past skin and bone and shields and walls, to locate the person she kept hidden. Oh. The way he wore a pair of jeans and the sound of his laugh. The scent of his skin.

Earlier, before he'd changed out of his food-splattered clothes, she still had that roar of recognition, want and desire swim into and heat her blood. That told her a lot. Ryan—the man he was, inside and out—resonated with her deeply. Intensely. On all levels.

I love you, Ryan.

Andrea swallowed the sigh of yearning with the last bite of her cake. Leaning forward, she set her plate on the coffee table, on top of Ryan's empty one, and said, "Well. Maybe we didn't have the evening you thought we would, but I have loved every second."

"Me, too," Ryan said. "Thank you for…being you. And jumping in to lend a hand."

"You're welcome." Should she leave? Was the evening over? She wasn't ready to go, didn't want the night to come to an end, but without some type of a hint from Ryan, she didn't know what to do. Why not just ask? "Are you ready for me to take off?"

Lines creased his forehead. "What? No, Andi." He reached for and clasped her hand. "I am absolutely, unequivocally *not* ready for you to take off. Where did you get that idea?"

"It wasn't an idea, exactly," she said, enjoying his touch. "I just wanted to know."

"Well, now you do."

"Now I do." Easing herself a few inches in his direction, she ran her other hand down his arm and delighted when his muscles tensed below her touch. "It seems so strange to think we've only known each other since June," she said. "I mean, how is that possible?"

"I wondered the same at first, but then decided the whys weren't important. To me," he said, rubbing his thumb in small circles in the palm of her hand, "the fact we feel this way at all is what counts. What we should respect and value and pay attention to."

"Hmm. I like how you put together words. You always sound so wise."

"Yeah?" A throaty rumble of laughter rolled from his chest. "Thank you. I'm not sure I agree but can accept your take without putting up an argument."

"Good," she said, happy to be snuggled close to Ryan. "Because you would lose."

"Maybe. Maybe not." A long sigh emerged. "We need to have a conversation. Several, in fact, but one should come before the other. And I'm not entirely positive how you'll take this."

"Oh?" On the edge of bliss one second and nervous—almost scared—the next. "Go on, then."

"We talked about Greg. I need to tell you about Leah."

"Leah?" Adding two plus two, Andi said, "A past girlfriend?"

"An ex-fiancée, actually." Ryan spoke slowly, methodically. "She was my client initially, for close to a year. We started dating about three months after the professional relationship ended. And yes, I had some concerns. I chose to trust in the positive."

Whoa. Ryan had loved another woman enough to propose? And that woman—Leah—had been his client? Oh, Lord. This wasn't good. None of it felt good. Or okay. Or manageable.

Ripples of panic she hadn't experienced in…weeks now, pushed at the fringes. Andi breathed. Planted her feet on the carpet and breathed again. She was fine. She was shocked, yes. Concerned, yes. But fine. When her affirmations became reality, she found her voice. "What happened? Why did the engagement end?"

Pivoting toward her, Ryan said, "She realized that while she loved me, she wasn't in love with me. This was about three years ago. Shortly after the breakup, I moved here."

Despite the nausea bouncing around in Andi's stomach, she also felt for this prior version of Ryan. For the guy who had lost the woman he'd planned on making his wife. "I'm sorry. That had to have been difficult, for both of you."

"It hurt then, as it should have." He shrugged, as if shaking off a fly. "Broken hearts are painful, for everyone involved. But she made the right decision, Andi.

We've stayed in contact, sporadically, ever since. Mostly via Facebook, but a phone call every now and again."

"I see." He'd fallen in love with a client. Now he was in a relationship with her. A pattern or coincidence? "And? Is there more?"

"Earlier this summer, she wrote me," Ryan said, in that same slow and methodical manner. "Said she might have made a mistake in ending our engagement, and wanted to know if I'd be willing to talk about the possibility of giving us another chance, to see if those feelings could be rekindled."

Oh, yeah, this just got better and better. Andi's heart dropped to her toes and sweat beaded on the back of her neck. On the heels of that, the fierce need to protect Ryan roared to life. Going with the latter emotion, she said, "Really? Three years after calling it quits, she suddenly has a change of heart? Again, I guess?"

"She was lonely, I think. Looking for a connection. I explained we had both moved on and that I had no wish to give us another shot. That I believe her original decision was correct."

"Okay. Thank you for telling me."

"Don't do that, Andi," Ryan said, cupping her cheeks with his hands. His touch was warm and solid. Secure. "Don't back away. What are you thinking? What's in that head of yours?"

"The truth?" Lord, what did she think? "I'm worried, I guess, that this is a pattern. Have you had relationships with other clients in addition to Leah and…me?"

"No. I haven't. And, come on, you were my client for a matter of weeks, not close to a year." Ryan stroked his fingers into her hair. "You can't really compare the two, sweetheart."

"But this…what happened with Leah is exactly what I'm afraid of, and now, there's more to worry about." Shivering, Andi wrapped her arms around herself. "In addition to my side, I have to wonder about your side. If…everything between us has any basis in reality. In authenticity. Or if we're both fooling ourselves for different reasons."

"I can't speak for you, but…listen to me, Andi. Just listen, okay?"

Tears that still hadn't escaped their prison except in her imaginary conversation with Hugh built behind her eyes. Heavy and uncomfortable. Painful. "Okay."

"I like your mind," Ryan said, speaking quickly. His voice was a blend of strength and surety, determination and emotion. "It's smart and funny and polite and kind. I like your heart. It's filled with grace and care and warmth and passion. I adore your beautiful and pure soul."

She might have, probably would have, argued with his poetic and angelic description—because really, she was an average woman with a normal heart and soul—but the facts of his relationship with Leah, her own fears and, yes, the powerful response her heart insisted on having due to that very same description left her…mute. Vulnerable. Confused.

So. Freaking. Confused.

"My mind is drawn to your mind. My heart to your heart. My soul to your soul. But, baby," Ryan said, his mouth near her ear, "it doesn't stop there. Because my body is also drawn to your body. Your vibrant, wild hair. The delicious length of your legs. The curve of your hips and, Lord, that ridiculously sexy mouth. You call to me, in every possible way, and that was not the case with Leah. Never has been with anyone else. Only you."

Sitting straight, Andi pulled herself free and, mostly due to the strong mix of emotions swamping her body, smoothed the skirt of her dress. It gave her something to do. A menial task to focus on, so maybe, just maybe, she could stop feeling so damn much.

What was she to do? How was she to know?

"You see too much in me, I think," she finally said. "And I won't deny that your mind, body, heart and soul call to me, too. But this…this is too difficult for me to define. It was cloudy before, Ryan, but now I'm… blinded. I can't see through to the other side."

And she refused to be rushed or talked into anything. For both of them, she refused to err in something so vitally important. His heart. Hers. Trust and love and belief.

"Just jump, baby. I'll catch you, and together we'll figure it out."

Huh. Just jump? "I can't do that, Ryan. I… Not now, at least. I think the best decision, the only practical decision, is to…step away. Get some air. Give us both a chance to consider if what we think we feel is real. Or just a figment of our overactive imaginations."

"I love you, Andrea," Ryan said. "I love you more today than I did yesterday, and I will love you more tomorrow than I do right this instant. I have no doubts on this."

I love you, too, Ryan. But did she?

"I need to leave now," she said. "I need to go somewhere I can think and process and wait for the confusion to fade. Because, Ryan, I can't see the truth."

"Maybe you need to stop searching so hard," he said,

looking tired and drained and so very…defeated. She'd never seen him that way before. "Maybe you need to trust your heart, trust me and, like I said…just jump. I'll be here, Andrea. When and if you're ready to take that step. A day, a week, a month or a year. I'll wait. You're that important. I'm that sure."

He didn't try to stop her and he didn't say anything more, but that was Ryan. Living up to his promises, his word. And he'd always said that whatever happened between them was in her control. So she nodded and slipped on her sandals, grabbed her purse and walked out of Ryan Bradshaw's house. Away from the best man she'd ever known. Would probably ever know.

A man who had brought her to life again with his patience and kindness and care. A man who had helped her step from the darkness, due to the light that surrounded him.

The only man she'd ever felt so strongly for.

And doing so? It hurt. It burned and twisted in her blood, knotted and shredded her stomach, and almost—*almost*—brought her to her knees. But she didn't cry. She remained one hundred percent dry-eyed for the drive to her aunt and uncle's. And for the entire night, as she stared at the ceiling while Ryan's words repeated themselves, over and over, in her brain.

I love you, Andrea. Just jump, baby. I'll catch you.

Chapter Eleven

October in Steamboat Springs marked the beginning of the busy ski season, which typically gave Ryan plenty of reasons to smile. He loved to ski and, ever since making his home here, would get out on the slopes whenever the opportunity presented itself. This year, though, he had no interest in his beloved sport. Hell. Truth was, he had no interest in anything.

The scenery outside his window? He'd stopped seeing and appreciating the breathtaking view. Food had lost its flavor. The rich, wake-up-and-start-the-day smell of brewing coffee no longer appealed or made his mouth water. Most mornings, directly opposite his prior behavior, he hit the snooze a total of three times before dragging his sorry behind out of bed.

All he saw when he closed his eyes was Andi. All he thought of when he woke was Andi. Sometimes, he thought he saw her when he was out and about. The briefest glimpse of red hair in the distance always sent his heart racing. She—her coconut-lime scent, the milky white skin, the sound of her laugh, the memory of her smile—followed him around. Everywhere.

Yet, she hadn't physically been in the state since near the end of August. And, Lord, he missed her with a ferocious ache that never dissipated. It existed in his heart, his soul, his mind and, yup, his body. If he'd needed more proof of his love, the ache of her loss would've done the trick.

But, no, he did not require additional proof.

At least today was Saturday, which meant he could hole up by himself without forcing smiles or good cheer or conversation. Here, he could be as damn miserable as he chose, thank you very much. And his plan was to do just that: sink to his eyeballs in misery, stay there for a solid twenty-four hours and then…no more of this insanity. She'd left his house that night without so much as a glance over her shoulder on her way out the door. They had a quick, strained conversation before she left Colorado and that was it. They hadn't talked since.

So yeah. As of tomorrow, he'd start living again.

Eventually, the line between real and pretend would fade, and he'd wake one morning a hell of a lot closer to his old self. Until then, he'd forge ahead with the same purpose he always had. Perhaps with the lingering hope that Andi would unexpectedly arrive at some point, having finally reached her place of clarity, ready and willing to jump with the trust that he'd open his arms wide and catch her before she fell. He would *always* be ready for that moment.

Ryan rolled to his side and stared at the clock. Considered taking a shower, brushing his teeth, making a late breakfast since it was already ten and…quickly decided he'd rather stay put and close his eyes. Pretend that Andrea was curled next to him, safe and snug and…

happy. Yeah. He liked that plan. Seemed a good enough way to spend another hour, maybe two.

Or the entire friggin' day.

Closing his eyes, he pulled in the image, the scent, the *feel* of the woman he loved and almost instantly felt a modicum of relief. That made it easy to stay right where he was and keep his eyes firmly shut. He might have dozed, he wasn't sure, but suddenly a blast of noise—a voice and a loud clanking—slammed into his ears with the force of a semi. Oh. Hell. No.

He did not bother opening his eyes, just yelled, "Go away, Nicole!"

She kept right on yelling at him to get up. Now. And banging on…well, he'd have to open his eyes to see exactly what was making that obnoxious noise, and that was something he refused to do. Yanking the pillow from the other side of the bed, he shoved it over his face in a weak attempt to block the skull-cracking, brain-bleeding sounds filling his bedroom.

All at once the deafening roar of noise disappeared. Thank the good Lord. "Nic, I love you," he said through the pillow, "but I'm pretty sure you just damaged my eardrums, my brain and very possibly a handful of other necessary body parts. Do that again and I'll—"

"Obviously, my dear brother, you are even more obstinate that I thought possible," Nicole said, in a sweet and loving way. Lies. She was here to add to his misery. "I'm moving on to step two of my plan. If you'd like to avoid this step, I suggest you get out of that bed."

"Ah. What's step two?"

"Roscoe is tied up outside right now, and he's in such a great mood," she said with the ego and humor of someone about to get their way. "I just took him for a walk. A nice long one, too, through the woods. And you know how much he adores rolling in the dirt. And he loves you. Why, he'll probably jump right on the bed and give you all sorts of wet, sticky kisses and—"

"Damn it," he muttered, knowing what Nicole knew. She had him. He loved dogs, even loved Roscoe, but that dog was clumsy and exuberant and…apparently covered in mud at this very second. "Why'd you bring Roscoe? Bursting my eardrums not enough for you?"

"Because he loves you! Almost as much as he loves me." He felt the bed shift as his sister sat down. "And come on, he's my ace in the hole. You'll do whatever I want if I keep Roscoe outside or promise to clean him before bringing him in."

Giving up the fight, Ryan pushed the pillow to the side and looked into his sister's concerned blue eyes. "I'm okay," he said. "Or I will be. No need for the theatrics."

"Okay, sure," she said. "No more theatrics. How about we talk, instead? Because baby brother, I've never seen you like this. And we're all worried."

"It's called a broken heart, Nic. It happens. They heal, mine will, too."

"Yeah, of course, but I think it's time for the Bradshaw determination to make an appearance. And I have some ideas on the proactive front." Winking, Nicole held her hand toward him. "Come on, Ry-Ry, go take a shower and I'll fix us some food. And then we'll talk, see what we can come up with to win back your love."

Hmm. He considered arguing with her, because really, he didn't want to intrude on Andrea's life. She knew exactly where he was. Exactly how to get a hold of him. But hell. If he didn't do as Nicole asked, that darn dog of hers would be rolling around on his bed shortly.

"Fine," he said. "But no promises. We'll have a conversation. I'll consider your ideas, and then you'll leave. Whatever I do then is my call. And sis? You're returning my house key."

She stuck out her tongue, as if she were six years old and left him alone. Yeah, she was something, his sister. And while he wouldn't admit it, regardless of what her so-called ideas were, the merest possibility of having a plan of action reignited his hope.

Albeit, the thinnest, most frayed strand of hope ever to exist. But, hey, it was there.

Andrea kept her gaze downward as she made her way to the elevator on the fourth floor of Juliana Memorial Hospital. She'd returned to work almost two months ago, but rather than taking her prior position in the trauma department—which had proved too difficult a task to undertake—she had asked for and received a transfer to maternity.

Honestly, she thought most folks were relieved.

While waiting for the elevator, Andi stretched her neck to one side and then the other. She'd worked an all-night shift and was ready—more than ready—to crawl into bed and sleep. Where she would think of Ryan. Dream of Ryan. Consider, again, her feelings and why she still found it so difficult to push past that last remaining wall and stop doubting all she felt.

All that he said he felt. Still felt. For her.

In the months that had passed since she'd left Steamboat Springs, not a day—often, not an hour—elapsed where Ryan evaded her thoughts. He was just always there, lingering about, almost as if her brain was set on reminding her that he waited. Returning to Rhode Island had been tough. There were so many instances since being home that she'd almost reached out with a phone call or a Facebook message or a text, but her worries pulled her back. Each and every time.

Until a Saturday evening in early October when he'd written her a short message: I miss you, Andi. You don't have to reply, but I wanted you to know this. I hope you're good. Happy. And still feeling alive. I so want you to feel alive. And remember there's this guy in Colorado who is waiting. Patiently. With his arms wide open.

She'd replied in an equally short and sweet manner, and before she knew it, they were messaging every day. In less than two weeks, they were talking on the phone, and by week three…she couldn't wait for those minutes and hours they would steal to be together. And, oh, had they talked. About everything and anything under the sun.

Except for how she felt. He never asked, and since she hadn't yet cleared the last shimmer of fog, she kept the topic closed. But she missed him and his smile and his sunlight. The crinkle around his eyes and the line of his jaw. The sensation of being wrapped tight in his embrace and the heat of their kisses. Yes, she missed him to the point of yearning.

But even now, with Christmas around the corner, she couldn't quite fall into the season of miracles. Because the idea of jumping with the hope that he'd catch her— metaphorically, of course—still filled her with numbing, freezing uncertainty. And that? It didn't make sense or hold any logic whatsoever. What she felt for Ryan was not based on the short time frame he'd professionally cared for her. This was no longer a question. This was what she *knew*.

No. The love she had for Ryan existed solely because of the unique chemistry they shared. Yet, the words *I love you* continually stuck in her throat like a wadded-up piece of gluey paper. Her lips would not form the words her heart and soul so wanted her to say.

The elevator finally reached her floor and the doors swung open. Inside, she pushed the garage-level button and leaned against the wall, breathed. So, with the caregiver-patient problem erased from her worries, what in the hell was the holdup? If only she knew. Or really, if she could somehow deduce the area where the problem resided, she'd take that as a win.

Absently, Andi rubbed her thigh, trying to relax the tightness, the slight muscle twinge that now only occurred after these all-night shifts. In nearly all ways, she'd regained her strength and mobility and, unless she was fatigued and overtired, didn't even walk with a limp. A year ago, she'd been…oh. A year? Yanking her phone from her pocket, Andrea stared at the date in shock. How had she not thought of this once all night? Yesterday, she'd remembered.

One year, to the day, since the shooting. A full twelve months—365 days.

Apprehension, stark fear, shivered and rolled through her limbs, raising goose bumps and lodging a golf-ball-size lump in her throat. And in a split second of pure understanding, of unhindered self-awareness, Andrea knew what she had to do.

The only thing she *could* do.

Today of all days, she needed to pay tribute to what had occurred. To the pain and the fear and the losses. And while she would rather pull out her hair one strand at a time than proceed forward, she went ahead and pushed the "1" button on the elevator panel. She needed to do this. For herself, for Hugh, for the 911 operator who'd saved her life…and everyone else involved in the tragedy.

Gathering every ounce of her strength and courage, Andrea straightened her spine—pretended it was formed of steel—and when the elevator doors opened, stepped out and into the hallway that would lead her to the trauma department. And as she walked the path she'd done so very often in the past, she thought about the horror. Her overriding terror and excruciating pain. The stench and the sounds. The people who had died, those who had lived. She thought about *him*: the man who'd lost his wife, and then shortly after, his sanity. The gunman.

As she arrived at the wide, double-door entry to the unit, she said a prayer, breathed in as deeply and as fully as possible, imagined Ryan's hand on her shoulder and, once she'd punched the large silver pad to open the doors, forced her legs to carry her forward. As if of their own accord, they took her to the break room first, where she had sat and joked with Hugh.

Precious minutes never to be returned.

Emotion welled behind her eyes. She ignored the burning, heavy pressure and continued on, following the same path she had one year ago. Now, the sounds and scents and terror didn't require her to call them forth, they were just there. Fresh and alive and real. Present day faded into the background, and suddenly it was as if she had truly stepped back in time.

Like her nightmare, but different. Because this was her choice. Her decision.

At the nurses' station, she gripped the counter and squeezed so tightly her knuckles whitened. A slight pivot to her right showed the spot where she had stood when two bullets tore into her leg and she went down. And, oh, God. There. Right there, straight ahead and on the other end of the long counter that made up the nurses' station, was…Hugh. Phantom Hugh, brought forth by her memories. Standing in the place he'd last breathed, last smiled.

And those damn broken tears of hers grew heavier. Stronger. More vicious as her sorrows and regrets and anger merged together, creating a…monster of sorts.

He looked so good to her aching heart, so she just soaked him in, this kind and intelligent man who had been her friend, her best mentor. Gray hair, brushed backward to hide his hated balding spot. Wire-rimmed glasses. Perfectly pressed pants and…a Looney Tunes necktie. How had she forgotten that? Shaking her head, Andi took a careful step forward.

Just one. If she moved too fast, he might just disappear. And she wasn't ready to never see him like this again. Alive and real and happy. Oh, he looked so happy. He had a thick-stacked clipboard in his left hand, a pen in his right and, when he saw her, that quirky, lovable smile. She opened her mouth, then and now, to tease him about overburdening the nurses when everything went to hell. One minute, all was calm. The next, bedlam.

A shot, then another, rang out. And then…Hugh's

stricken expression. The blood pouring from his stomach as he collapsed. As she had on that day one year ago, she ran forward, her only intent to help. To be there for Hugh. Only this time, she wasn't shot. Pain did not magnify and pulse through her leg. She made it all the way to him. Kneeling down, she reached toward Hugh, already uttering words of encouragement, of care, and he...vanished.

"No," she whispered, staring hard at the now-empty floor. "Give me one more chance to do this right. Just one." But no, nothing. Hugh was gone. Forever gone. She wouldn't, couldn't, change the past despite her intense desire to do so. What had happened, happened.

It was then that her tears, after a year of stubborn, painful silence, finally fell. They ran down her cheeks in a rushing stream, dripped into her mouth and off her jaw, and they kept on coming. A year's worth of pain being shed all at once. Made sense, she supposed, in a convoluted sort of way. And that was fine. Let the tears fall.

Andrea leaned against the nurses' station and didn't attempt to halt or slow or silence her gulping sobs. She let them out. She gave them control. They crawled from the deepest recesses of her heart and soul, from where the most desperate of her pain resided, and as they did, she reveled in the freedom. The wonderful treasure of being able to cry.

One of the nurses handed her a box of tissues, which she accepted. And for the next long, long while, Andi did nothing but cry. When she'd expunged the last tear, when her clogged-up emotions from the past twelve months were finally released, another wall dropped and gave way. Bam. Gone. *Forever* gone. And this, unlike losing Hugh, was a precious gift.

"I love you, Ryan," she whispered. "I'm about to jump, so get ready."

Chapter Twelve

Whistling a Christmas carol, Ryan finished stringing the blinking white lights on the tree and, after a moment's hesitation, went to prepare a simple meal of grilled cheese and tomato soup. He'd finish decorating the tree after he ate and, hopefully by then, he would have heard from Andi. Today—the one-year anniversary of the hospital shooting—had to be taking its toll.

And he was worried.

During their phone conversations over the past few days, she'd been reserved and quiet. Easy to guess the reason for her distance, but she hadn't said a whole lot on the matter. If she was here, with him, he'd have tried harder to get her to talk. Too many miles existed between them, though, and without the ability to see her eyes and read her body language—hold her tight if the need arose—he refused to push such a sensitive, emotional topic.

Ryan took his dinner to the living room, setting both the plate and the bowl on the coffee table. Checked his phone to see if he'd somehow missed a call or a message—he hadn't—and let out a long sigh. Damn, he hoped she was okay. Wished he could be there instead of here.

Or vice versa. Either would do the trick.

Since neither was the case, and worrying wouldn't solve the dilemma, he turned his thoughts toward Christmas and the few remaining gifts he'd yet to purchase.

His sister's being the top of the list. Typically, they went the funny route in the gifts they exchanged, for birthdays and Christmas. But this year, she deserved— had earned—the perfect serious and heartfelt present from him. She hadn't allowed him to remain stuck in the muck. And while he'd have eventually gotten around to contacting Andi without Nicole's obnoxious pestering, she had shortened the gap by, at a minimum, a month.

But Nicole, with her stubborn attitude, muddy dog and his friggin' *best* stockpot—which she'd smacked on relentlessly with a stainless steel spoon—had yanked him clean from the trenches. And he couldn't forget the combination of his sister's genuine compassion and creative nature, either. Or for that matter, the determination they'd both inherited from their father.

All of the above had come into play, had served as a wake-up call. And for those reasons, he would remain forever grateful and—to Nicole's complete delight— eternally in her debt. Since he'd written Andi that first message, they'd slowly rebuilt their foundation, one brick at a time, and in his opinion, they were gaining ground daily. As friends. As a couple. As partners.

He told her he loved her, often, with the reassurance that he didn't expect her to return the sentiment until—or *if*, he supposed—she chose to. But that *his* choice was to make damned sure that Andrea knew every single day that she was loved. By him. And that he was still here, waiting and ready to catch her, if she ever decided to take that leap.

Would she? Honestly, he didn't have a clue. To assume she would or wouldn't boiled down to wasted energy, and he far preferred to sit in the moment and enjoy every second they spent together, whether in emails or texts or on the phone. Each one of these seconds offered a deeper, truer glimpse into the woman he loved. Was it all he wanted?

Oh, hell, no. But until or unless she decided otherwise, it was enough. Had to be enough, because there would never be another Andi. For Ryan, she was his once-in-a-lifetime woman.

Another glance at his phone showed no new messages, no missed calls. Try to call her again? Send her another message? *No.* Not yet. He'd give her a few more hours first.

With dinner done, Ryan returned to the kitchen, rinsed off his dishes and put them in the dishwasher. Checked his phone and swallowed his concerns. She was fine. Of course, she was. Hell. As far as he knew, her family and friends had made plans for the night. She could be at the movies or soaking up to her chin in a bubble bath or… lying on her bed, crying.

Okay. He'd send her another message, let her know of his concerns, and—

The sharp ring of the doorbell interrupted his thoughts and, because he wasn't expecting anyone, sent a quick bolt of shock through his system. Could be his parents, he supposed, as they had taken to dropping in a lot more often as of late. Or his sister, though he'd have known if she was visiting. And with Christmas a week away, since she'd be here then, that seemed unlikely.

Ryan swung open the front door and…stopped breathing. Stopped thinking. His blood stopped circulating in his veins, and every muscle in his body froze. His jaw went slack.

"Are you going to invite me in or let me freeze to death?" Andi asked, a wide smile wreathed across her face. "Because it's snowing out here and it's cold. And windy. After three planes and two layovers, I'm also starving, thirsty and...are you okay?" Her eyes narrowed as she looked at him. "Ryan? Hello? You're not moving. At all."

The sound of her voice eased in, warmed his blood and revved his heart. Andrea was here, without any warning or advance notice. On the one-year anniversary of the worst moment of her life. What did that mean? It certainly meant something. Good or bad or...something.

It had to be good. Otherwise, why deal with three planes and two layovers?

"I'm fine," he said, finding his volume. His hope. "Surprised to see you, is all."

"Wouldn't have been any fun if I'd warned you."

"There is that." Stepping aside, he grinned. "God, it's good to see you."

Other than a smile, she offered no response. Just breezed right by him and was well into the living room before he'd even closed the door. Huh. Okay. All of this seemed positive. So. Damn. Positive. But he hadn't forgotten the night she'd left—as quickly as she'd now appeared—and the devastating effect her absence had wrought. On him. His heart. His soul.

Perhaps he wasn't as okay with the status quo as he'd believed.

Dragging in a steadying breath, he followed Andi's footsteps and stopped. Frozen for the second time in a very few minutes. And, yup, his jaw weakened, his ability to take in air disappeared, and his brain halted all thought processes as he took in the scene in front of him.

What was this woman—*his woman*—up to?

Whatever it was, she obviously had some sort of plan in mind and had gotten right to it. She'd taken off her coat, had draped it over the back a chair, and was presently arranging two of the sofa cushions—side by side—on the kitchen floor, right in front of the center island. Standing, she tossed her glorious hair behind her shoulders and grinned. Again, widely. Happily.

Behind that smile, though, lurked an interesting mix of nerves, excitement and humor. The three ignited the same in Ryan, along with his curiosity. His pleasure in…her. Lord, he loved this woman. To the stars and the moon and back, and yeah, back again.

"Ah…Andi?" he asked, unable to help himself. "Whatcha doing?"

She tugged at the waistband of her forest-green sweater, which had ridden up just enough to glimpse a few delectable inches of bare skin, and shrugged. "You'll see. I'm almost ready."

Ready? Hmm. "I don't know what you're up to," he said, "but you're amazing."

"I hope you still feel that way in a few minutes."

"I will." Without doubt. Sticking his thumbs in the front pockets of his jeans, he leaned against the wall, intent on watching—just watching—the beauty of Andrea in motion.

She went to the kitchen island, her movements fluid and, in a systematic fashion, emptied its surface. The bowl of fruit, the cutting board, the folded dish towel and the knife block found a new home on the counter right next to the sink. "Okay," she murmured. "That should do it."

"Should do what, exactly?" he asked. "I have to admit to some confusion."

"Good," she said with a cute little smirk. Crossing to him, she grasped his hands and tugged. Sure, he'd play along. With anything this woman had in mind. They walked a few feet, in tandem, and she positioned him behind the sofa cushions. "Stand here. Don't argue."

"Wouldn't think of it, baby. I'm yours. To do with as you will."

She walked to the island, kicked off her shoes. Before Ryan could so much as blink, she was sitting on the surface of the island. Another second later, she'd pulled herself to her feet and stood taller than him by a decent margin. And, Lord, he *knew* what she was doing. Surprising, really, that it had taken him this long to catch on. Yup. This woman? His. *All his.*

Damn lucky is what he was. The most fortunate man on earth.

Brown eyes—soft and serious and warm—met his. "This is what's happening," she said, her tone steady. Sure. "You're going to open your arms and I'm going to jump. If you catch me, well…then, I'm yours—" her voice wavered, just a little "—forever. You good with that?"

"Yes, baby. Absolutely and without any doubt whatsoever." And while he had every intention in the world of catching her, holding her as close to him as possible, and then kissing those lips of hers for a very, very long time, he had to ask, "What if I don't catch you? You must have some doubts or you wouldn't have bothered with the soft, cushiony landing."

"Oh," she said with a quirk of an eyebrow, "that's simple. If you don't catch me, then you're mine. Forever. And every single day, for the rest of our lives, I get to remind you that you let me fall. But that I—the wondrous woman I am—still chose you over anyone else."

"I see," he said, somehow loving her more by the second. "Every day, huh?"

"Maybe more than once a day, even. I think that's fair, don't you?"

"I don't know," he said, joining in on the teasing. "Could we renegotiate, possibly?"

"Uh-uh." Angling her arms across her chest, she said, "This deal is firm."

"Alrighty, then. I agree." Slowly, he lifted his arms and opened them wide. Hoping that in his eyes she could see the love he had for her, he said, "I'm right here, baby."

One blink. Two. "Forever, Ryan. I'm not joking with this."

"Me, either. Trust in that. Trust in us and just…jump."

A third blink, a quick nod and, bending her knees slightly, Andi jumped. Toward him and his waiting arms instead of bolting and running in the opposite direction. He stepped forward and, as her body crashed into his, he wrapped his arms around her, bringing her to his chest. Tight. Secure. Her hair, soft and sensuous, brushed against his jaw, and her scent—cinnamon instead of coconut—rushed his senses. She laughed, loudly and joyously, and for a second, he thought they were home free. But then, in trying to keep his balance, his foot slid. They tumbled.

And they fell together, landing in a heap with him on the floor and her body plastered on top of his. Again, their gazes met, and in Andi's eyes he saw laughter and love and an entire lifetime of both ahead of them. "You let me fall," she said softly. "How could you do that?"

"*We* fell. But I caught you first," he said, lost in her scent, the warmth—the *reality*—of her. Of a moment he would never, ever forget. "And I'd like to point out that I am still holding you. I never let go, baby. I never will. I promise you this, Andrea."

Time stilled for one beat, two beats, three beats of his heart. "I love you, Ryan Bradshaw," Andrea said quietly. Reverently. "I'm sorry—so, so sorry—that it took me this long to say these words, to embrace what we have—what we've always had—but I'm here now. Here forever. I will never run from you again."

The words weren't necessary. Not anymore, but he couldn't deny the relief that hearing them brought. Or the certainty in her voice. He'd known the truth so early on—that from cell to bone to blood, this woman belonged with him, to him, and he belonged with her, to her—and he'd never doubted this. Not once. But yes, that she now knew the same, and believed and was willing to risk it all for him, for them and their future meant…everything.

Everything in the world that mattered, anyway.

"I love you, too, Andrea Caputo. Fiercely. Devotedly. Completely. With all I am today, all I'll be tomorrow. More than you'll ever know. More than I can ever fully express." Emotion, strong and pressing, deepened his voice. "Thank you, baby, for taking that jump."

"You're welcome." She grazed his jaw with soft, sweet kisses. "Thank you, too. For never giving up or growing impatient. For catching me and holding on tight."

Feathering his fingers into her hair, he drew her closer and kissed her with all of the hunger, desire and passion he had for this woman and only this woman. Contentment stole in, riding along with the fire in his blood, hand in hand, that he would never again have to go a day in his life without Andrea by his side. They were a team. Meant for each other.

And, really, what else could a man want but his other half?

Well. One thing, maybe. "Baby?" he said, breaking the kiss. "I have this…let's call it a strong desire to pick you up and haul you to my bed. Now, as in this minute. Where I intend on having my way with you… with every inch of you. I'm hoping you're good with that prospect?"

A sultry, sexy, *hot* laugh emerged. "Sure, but only if I then get to have my way with…ah…every inch of your body. I mean, that's only fair, right?"

"I'd say that's more than fair." And with that, he lifted the love of his life, the woman who called to his heart, soul, head and body, into his arms and carried her to his bed.

Where he planned on keeping both of them busy for a good, long while.

Epilogue

Today, in less than twenty minutes, Andrea Caputo would walk down the aisle and become Ryan's wife. Incredible to think that this time a year ago—last October—she had been ensconced at home in Rhode Island, still attempting to locate that seed of peace, to understand why she couldn't voice the powerful love she had for her now soon-to-be husband.

Incredible, too, what had happened in the trauma center when she'd finally cried. Finally was able to fully let go of the past, embrace the present and catch a glimpse of the beautiful future that awaited her with Ryan. She'd loved him long before that day, but she couldn't express that to him or to herself without first confronting what she so yearned to change.

Peace had entered her soul as she'd cried and, with that peace, her ability to go to Ryan and take that leap into his waiting arms. Odd, really, how the brain and heart functioned. Sometimes in tandem and other times, in seeming discord. Yet…they were inexorably connected. One had to be in accord with the other in order to feel whole.

Not so different, really, than what she had with Ryan.

They were okay on their own, could possibly even reach great, but together? They were magnificent.

The man she loved had surprised her with a romantic proposal at their hot spring last June, on the anniversary of when they'd met. Naturally, she'd said yes before he'd even gotten the complete question out of his mouth. How could she not?

Ryan was…the sun in her life, and she…his.

"It's time," Andrea's mother, Colleen, said from where she stood behind Andi. She'd been fussing with Andrea's hair for the past fifteen minutes. "And darling, you look so beautiful. Radiant and excited and in love. Just how a bride is supposed to on her wedding day."

"Thank you, Mom." Wow. This was really happening. Carefully, Andrea pivoted in a circle, watching her reflection in the mirror. The pale golden ankle-length skirt, a frothy concoction of layers—reminding her of butterfly wings—rippled and fluttered around her legs, making her feel…glorious. And, okay, a lot like the sun. The bodice of the gown had a sweetheart neckline, and there the fabric was a soft, silky white. "I…guess I'm ready."

Together, they left Andrea's bedroom and proceeded through her aunt and uncle's home to the kitchen, where her father, Ken, and her sister, Audrey, waited. The marriage ceremony was to take place in the backyard, among the trees and their changing colors. Andi would've loved to marry Ryan at their hot spring, but there simply wasn't enough room. This had seemed the perfect alternative. The place Ryan had first made her laugh.

"Told you, Dad," Audrey said, smiling. "She's an angel today."

Ken Caputo placed his hand on his heart and, with damp eyes, said, "Look at you, sweetheart, all grown up and…so beautiful. How'd this happen so fast? I swear, you were three years old just yesterday, begging for shoulder rides and ice-cream sundaes."

"Aw, Dad. Don't make me cry!" Standing on her tiptoes, Andrea kissed her father on the cheek and then, whispering into his ear, said, "You're the first man I ever loved, Daddy. You're the benchmark. You showed me what to look for in the man I chose to marry."

"Who is making whom cry now?" he asked, his voice suspiciously thick. He rubbed his eyes with the back of his hand and then tucked her arm into his. "Everything is set, everyone is here. And I have to say, your groom? He's waiting on eggshells. Ready to do this, pumpkin?"

"Oh, yes," she said, her heart beating in a steady, comforting and confident rhythm. "Very much so. I don't want to keep anyone, but especially Ryan, waiting."

"Then let's do this."

Audrey handed Andi her bouquet of white roses and squeezed her hand. Then, following Audrey—Andi's only bridesmaid—they exited the house through the back door and started their path toward the white aisle runner that would lead her to Ryan. And, oh, the setting for the ceremony was lovely. Modest, yes, but…so very perfect in so many ways.

Rows of chairs were spread on either side of the aisle, filled with friends and family. Tree branches dipped and bobbed in the gentle breeze, every now and then sending a scattering of leaves floating downward. A haze of red and gold and yellow and green. At the end of the aisle, where Ryan waited, was a wedding arc that her male cousins had built for them.

Also simple and lovely. And yes, perfect, too.

The only downside—and really, not that much of one, because Andi refused to allow anything to detract from her joy—were the gray, puffy clouds hovering in the sky above, dimming the gentle glow of the sun. Even if it rained, the first drops weren't likely to fall until well after the ceremony, and the reception was planned for inside the house.

So, no. Gray clouds were not about to cast a shadow on the day she became Ryan's wife.

Reid, seeing them approach, started the wedding music, and in the space of a heartbeat Andi was stepping onto the aisle runner and walking toward the man who had awakened her heart and her soul. Who had seen right through her defensive shields to the real her, and then had done everything in his power to show her how well they fit.

Because he had known, right at the start, that they did, indeed, belong with each other.

He stood there now, tall and sure, with that smile she so adored, in dark gray dress slacks that were paired with a white shirt and a silver-gray vest. His hair ruffled in the light wind, and his glued-to-her gaze was serious. Intent and intense. And filled with enduring love.

For her. Only for her.

With Ryan, her future would include moments of joy and laughter, sadness and tears, love and passion, along with everything else that two people creating a life together brought to the table. There would be children down the road, more love and laughter and tears to be shared. As the years piled up on one another, there would be gray hairs and tired muscles, and wrinkles would form around their eyes and mouths, but this love they had for one another?

It would stick. It would grow. It would sit and settle and steam between them, for however many years they were graced. And she intended to cherish every damn second. From the awful to the average to the astounding—and she was certain that the astounding moments would vastly outnumber the rest—she would treasure them all.

This was her life. Her life with Ryan.

When she reached the aisle's halfway mark, the clouds just over Ryan's head broke and a bright ray of sunshine washed over him, blinding him enough that he squinted his eyes. She laughed, she couldn't help herself, because this man—*her* man—walked in the light of the sun.

And she was so ridiculously fortunate to be the woman to share his light.

* * * * *

MILLS & BOON®

Cherish™

EXPERIENCE THE ULTIMATE RUSH OF FALLING IN LOVE

A sneak peek at next month's titles...

In stores from 2nd June 2016:

- **His Cinderella Heiress** – Marion Lennox *and* **Marriage, Maverick Style!** – Christine Rimmer
- **The Bridesmaid's Baby Bump** – Kandy Shepherd *and* **Third Time's the Bride!** – Merline Lovelace

In stores from 16th June 2016:

- **Bound by the Unborn Baby** – Bella Bucannon *and* **His Surprise Son** – Wendy Warren
- **Wedded for His Royal Duty** – Susan Meier *and* **The BFF Bride** – Allison Leigh

Lynne Graham has sold 35 million books!

To settle a debt, she'll have to become his mistress...

Nikolai Drakos is determined to have his revenge against the man who destroyed his sister. So stealing his enemy's intended fiancé seems like the perfect solution! Until Nikolai discovers that woman is Ella Davies...

Read on for a tantalising excerpt from Lynne Graham's 100th book,

BOUGHT FOR THE GREEK'S REVENGE

'Mistress,' Nikolai slotted in cool as ice.

Shock had welded Ella's tongue to the roof of her mouth because he was sexually propositioning her and nothing could have prepared her for that. She wasn't drop-dead gorgeous... *he* was! Male heads didn't swivel when Ella walked down the street because she had neither the length of leg nor the curves usually deemed necessary to attract such attention. Why on earth could he be making *her* such an offer?

'But we don't even know each other,' she framed dazedly. 'You're a stranger...'

'If you live with me I won't be a stranger for long,' Nikolai pointed out with monumental calm. And the very sound of that inhuman calm and cool forced her to flip round and settle distraught eyes on his lean darkly handsome face.

'You can't be serious about this!'

'I assure you that I am deadly serious. Move in and I'll forget your family's debts.'

'But it's a *crazy* idea!' she gasped.

'It's not crazy to me,' Nikolai asserted. 'When I want anything, I go after it hard and fast.'

Her lashes dipped. Did he want her like that? Enough to track her down, buy up her father's debts, and try and buy rights to her and her body along with those debts? The very idea of that made her dizzy and plunged her brain into even greater turmoil. 'It's immoral... it's blackmail.'

'It's definitely *not* blackmail. I'm giving you the benefit of a choice you didn't have before I came through that door,' Nikolai Drakos fielded with a glittering cool. 'That choice is yours to make.'

'Like hell it is!' Ella fired back. 'It's a complete cheat of a supposed offer!'

Nikolai sent her a gleaming sideways glance. 'No the real cheat was you kissing me the way you did last year and then saying no and acting as if I had grossly insulted you,' he murmured with lethal quietness.

'You *did* insult me!' Ella flung back, her cheeks hot as fire while she wondered if her refusal that night had started off his whole chain reaction. What else could possibly be driving him?

Nikolai straightened lazily as he opened the door. 'If you take offence that easily, maybe it's just as well that the answer is no.'

MILLS & BOON®

The One Summer Collection!

Join these heroines on a relaxing
holiday escape, where a summer fling
could turn in to so much more!

Order yours at **www.millsandboon.co.uk/onesummer**